Moon Dance

Sleeps

Alien Encounters, Book 2

Jo Hammers

Paranormal Crossroads & Publishing

Moon Dance Sleeps

ISBN 978-0-9849879-8-6

www.paranormalcrossroads.com

This work is fiction. All of the characters, organizations, and events portrayed in this novel are either products of the author's imagination or are used fictitiously.

TABLE OF CONTENTS

Moon Dance Sleeps

Alien Encounters, Book 2

Jo Hammers

CHAPTER ONE

TIME TO GO HOME

Pansy Sky Walker, a half- breed Weelo, stood sweeping sand from the top of a sixteen foot piece of round metal buried beneath a sand dune. She was working fast and laboriously. In the distance, a great cloud was approaching the size of ten football fields. She was sure it was time to uncover the tribe's great secret, a hidden bullet shaped space craft hidden by them for thousands of years. They needed the air craft to fly up to the Mother Ship and board. The alien women of her tribe, hidden in the desert of New Mexico, were beings from planet Weelo and had survived for the last two or three hundred years as native American Indians roaming Canada, the United States, and Mexico.

In their tribe, there were pure Weelo and then there were children that were born to them with no Alien traits having taken after human mothers and fathers. Pansy Sky Walker was what earth men called a half breed. She was half Weelo and half white.

Pansy Sky Walker gave birth to a child named Carol Sue that she claimed to be Gray Feather's, the tribe's medicine man. Pansy, who had always been treated as a half breed by the tribe, had for the last three years been out for revenge in any way she could get it. Telling Moon Dance that her child was Gray Feather's was her ultimate scheme to get even with Moon Dance for taking Gray Feather from her.

Moon Dance could not accept Gray Feather's infidelity and was sure that she had been an old fool in thinking he could love her. Moon Dance was older than Gray Feather in human years. Gray Feather loved Moon Dance as much as she loved him, but unfortunate circumstances become a wedge between them.

Now, the Great Mother Ship was coming to rescue the pure Weelo after thousands of years. Those boarding the ship to return home to the planet Weelo had to be of pure lineage. Each pure lineage could take one earth human or half breed with them as a slave or human specimen to study.

Pansy Sky Walker was granted passage as Moon Dance's choice. The reason being, Pansy Sky Walker was the tribe's storyteller, a walking history book of the tribe's survival. Pansy and Moon Dance were enemies, but they would board together. Gray Feather, thinking that Moon Dance was dead, needed a pure Weelo to board with. He chose an older Weelo woman of influence and married her ensuring him boarding privilege.

Now it was time to board.

Pansy worked furiously trying to uncover their space craft. The Great Mother Ship, Noah II, was in the distant sky and approaching fast.

Gray Feather, the love of Moon Dance's life, had just returned after three years of absence from the tribe bringing two friends with him. One was named Jack Benson, a psychiatrist from New Jersey. Tribal legend said that when a man named Benson made his way to them, it would mark the day the Great Mother Ship would come. Tribal legend was correct. Pansy was sweeping with a frenzy trying to uncover the space ship from its hiding place in a dune of sand. As the tribe's storyteller, she hadn't really believed in the tribe's fairy tales till she saw the great cloud like craft coming and the appearance of Benson earlier in the day.

The first Great Mother Ship, Noah I, had crashed several thousands of years before. Its doctor was lost in a great flood having been washed overboard and down a river many miles. With broken bones, he couldn't make it back to the Great Mother and was forced to step down thru the centuries alone stepping from body to body, incarnating. No one knew the identity of the doctor as he had stepped down thru the centuries a part from the tribe, having been lost in the crash. The Weelo tribe in the desert of New Mexico had assumed for thousands of years that he was dead.

Now, Pansy Skywalker was a believer. Even though she was the tribe's storyteller, she hadn't really believed all the stories that had been handed down to her by her grandmother who was also a story teller. She was disgusted as she worked alone trying to unearth their space flyer. She always thought it was a bullet shaped travel trailer. Now, she knew better because she could see similar bullet shaped space craft flying in the sky above checking out the Great Mother Ship as it lowered in the sky.

The oblivious tribe had hurried off down the desert spring path to greet and welcome back their medicine man, Gray Feather. All the tribe loved him and was loyal to him. She, however, had mixed emotions. He had dumped her three years or so before for Moon Dance, a woman three times her age. Old wounds had laid silent in her waiting for the right moment for revenge. She hadn't chased down the path to grovel at his feet, nor had Moon Dance.

Pansy Skywalker had once tricked Gray Feather into sleeping with her so that Moon Dance saw. It was her revenge on Moon Dance for taking him away from her. However, she still hadn't had revenge for him dumping her. She was glad he was back and she planned to burn his ass when she got a chance. For now, however, she needed to get the space flyer ready to go. She continued to replay old hurtful memories as she worked uncovering the tribe's space craft.

The night Pansy Skywalker seduced Gray Feather; she was pregnant with another man's child. It had been sweet revenge to tell Moon Dance that her child belonged to Gray Feather. She had no intention of ever telling Moon Dance any difference. Carol Sue, her daughter, was over two years old. She had been a month pregnant when she slept with Gray Feather. The timing back then could not have been any more perfect.

Moon Dance had been the medicine woman and second highest ranking woman in the Weelo tribe three years before. The Weelo men had abandoned them in the desert and a new chain of command was set up necessary for survival. Moon Dance became the provider for the tribe of women as well as their doctor or medicine woman. Hissing Cat became chief and Leaping Lizard her assistant. Pansy had been demoted to laundress as well as story teller for the tribe. She did not see herself as anyone's maid.

Now the time had come and her three years of misery with the tribe and a child she didn't want was over. In Pansy's thinking, Moon Dance was an aging idiot. Why would a seventy year old respected Weelo woman chase a thirty year old medicine man and seriously think he was in love with her? There was no fool like an old fool and that included women in her thinking. After Gray Feather had abandoned her and Moon Dance, she had taken every opportunity to poke fun at Moon Dance pointing out her folly. She loved telling at campfires how their great medicine man, Gray Feather, had slept with her and given her the prettiest child ever born into the tribe. It was sweet rubbing her child, Carol Sue, in Moon Dance's face.

Gray Feather had told Pansy the night he slept with her that he was forever, deeply in love with Moon Dance. He tried to explain to Pansy that it was not Moon Dance's seventy year old body that he was in love with. It was the woman in her. Being dumped for a seventy year old hag of an Indian woman was hard to take. Pansy Skywalker was only in her twenties. She vowed never to tell Moon Dance that Gray Feather had made that statement. She wanted Moon Dance to think he had purposely betrayed her; sleeping with her and getting her pregnant. That was her revenge and it was sweet.

As Pansy swept off the top of the space craft, seventy- six year old Moon Dance joined her and started sweeping sand from one side of the flyer. There was no other way to uncover it.

"We must hurry Pansy Sky Walker. The great gray cloud in the distance is the Great Mother Ship. It will continue to look like a great, gray fog until it hovers above us. About twenty Earth minutes is all we will have to get the women on board this space craft and fly up to the ship and dock. The mother has to make other stops for the ancient ones in Utah and those of the North tribe up by the Canada line."

"It would have been nice if the other women had stayed here to help. They have run off to play footsy with Gray Feather at the spring. I am sure that you are aware that he is back and just as handsome as ever. You have aged. He has not." She stated trying to dig with her words like claws into the seventy- six year old, fragile Moon Dance who weighed less than a hundred pounds. At times, she had fed the tribe of women instead of feeding herself when food was short. She was in the worst condition physically of all the women.

"I have no intentions of resuming a friendship with Gray Feather or running to the spring to greet him." Moon Dance replied fighting back tears. Every inch of her body wanted to run to him. However, she could not. He had slept with Pansy Sky Walker and had a girl child by her. She would not play second fiddle to anyone. For Gray Feather to declare his love for her and then within twenty-four hours sleep and conceive a child by Pansy was the greatest disrespect there was. She had indeed been an old fool as Pansy Skywalker repeatedly said over the last three years. She had cried many tears out in the desert when she was alone and hunting snakes so that the tribe would have meat to eat.

Moon Dance had walked upon and saw Pansy in the arms of Gray Feather and him howling on the dune making love to her. She had watched in the shadows as he gave a child to Pansy. There was no greater disrespect. He had told her that he was madly in love with her and then went to bed with another before the midnight moon laughed. Gray Feather had shattered her heart.

"You are a fool Moon Dance. If the dark cloud is the Great Mother Ship com- ing, Gray Feather will make his way here ignoring you and me. On his arm will be one of the pure women of our tribe who will be willing to take him on board the Great Mother with them. He may be human, but he is a smart man. The Weelo civilization is so far advanced culturally and scientifically; he would be crazy not to go with us. He may be human, but he is a smart doctor and scientist."

"Who would disrespect me and take him on board?" Moon Dance asked sweep- ing with all of her strength. "Once we board the space flyer, I am the highest rank- ing Pure Weelo here."

"Look down the spring path. Your disrespect is headed our way with Gray Feather on her arm. Hissing Cat has taken off her mask to entice your love. She has blindsided you and I. She now owns Gray Feather! He has his hand where only the married men of our tribe put it."

Moon Dance climbed to the top of the dune which was still covering most of the space craft. She then put her hand above her eyes to shade them and allow her to look toward the spring. Pansy was not lying. Gray Feather was heading their way with Hissing Cat. The other women were following them and seemed to be celebrating. Moon Dance's heart felt like it was about to explode with jealousy as well as the pain. She was an old fool. Gray Feather walked with his hand on Hissing Cat's backside. When Weelo married they walked like that for the time of the wedding and reception so all could see that they were one. The impromptu women's celebration was a wedding party. It was the last straw for Moon Dance. She felt the light of her soul go out and decided she would not play second fiddle to Pansy or to Hissing Cat her adversary.

Moon Dance, with tears running down her face, took one last look out into the distance at the man she was in love with. Gray Feather's hand was on the backside of Hissing Cat and she was hanging all over him. Moon Dance burst into a flood of tears. Quickly, she half slid down the sand dune that covered the space craft to escape the approaching group. Taking the tail of her skirt, she dried her eyes quickly and then walked away heading for the burnt out Hogan which used to be her and Gray Feather's home. She would not wish him well on his marriage to Hissing Cat nor would she board the Great Mother Ship in disrespect and tears. The younger women had disrespected her by rejoicing over Gray Feather and Hissing Cat. She was thru. Her days, as provider and medicine woman, were over. She knew what the answer for her situation was. She would kill the body she lived in known as Moon Dance and find a new body and identity to assume. She would stay on Earth and possibly never go home. Maybe time and a new life would numb her Weelo heart. Her disrespectful tribe could go to Hell. She didn't feel she owed them anything.

"Where are you going?" shouted Pansy Sky Walker seeing that the huge gray cloud was getting closer in the distance.

"I will not be going home with you, Pansy Skywalker. You will dig me with your words no more. I am capable of surviving without you, the tribe, or Gray Feather. I will start a new tribe and it will not include any of you who have treated me so callously in this lifetime. I have been your provider and your medicine woman in a harsh land. My mission is complete. You can all now go to the white man's hell, as they say." Moon dance stated in anger walking away towards the Hogan.

"I will not miss you, Moon Dance!" Pansy yelled back wanting to dig her one last time. "Someday, Gray Feather will drop hissing Cat for me when he finds out I have bore him a child!"

Pansy was delighted that Moon Dance had a broken heart and was in tears just like she had once been when Gray Feather dumped her. "

Moon Dance hurried and made her way to the Hogan. She knew she didn't have much time before one of the younger women would come seeking her to board. She was the only one that was capable of flying the bullet shaped space flyer with any expertise. However, at the moment she did not give a damn. She would not lift a finger to help any of them. She was thru.

Moon Dance once again burst into tears as she entered and took one last look inside the Hogan where she had spent three years loving and caring for Gray Feather. She needed a brain fog like Gray Feather had once had. She needed so desperately to forget their good times together. Gray Feather had now married Hissing Cat. Pure Weelo were married forever unless they chose to set a human man's boots outside of their door divorcing him. Hissing Cat had been just as much in love with Gray Feather as she and Pansy Skywalker had been. Moon Dance's heart was crying and dying. It was time to choose a new life and move on. She would not command the space flyer with Hissing Cat and Gray Feather on board. She had her pride.

Exiting the Hogan door, she thought about the live Rattlesnake in the burlap bag just outside the Hogan door that she had caught for dinner. It was time for her to cease to be. She could not go home to her planet an old fool and be ridiculed by Pansy and Hissing Cat relentlessly for eternity. If Gray Feather had loved her, he would have made his way to her first, in spite of their differences. She was not first on his list. She was last which made her an old fool.

Walking over, she picked up her snake bag. The Rattlesnake inside of it began to move and hiss. Sitting down on the sand, she leaned on the Hogan wall and crossed her legs Indian fashion. Then she dumped the live, hot, mad snake out from the burlap bag and into her lap. Instantly the snake struck biting her on the side of the neck and then slithered away. Moon Dance did not fight the poison or to try to save herself, she leaned against the Hogan and let the venom have its way. She would exit her human body and choose a new body to enter somewhere else where no one knew her. She just had to wait for her human body to die and then she could exit it.

CHAPTER TWO

RESCUE SHIP

The Great Mother Ship was hovering overhead and the land was dark beneath in its shadow. Pansy Sky Walker watched as the returning women began to help frantically with the sweeping of sand from the bullet shaped space craft. The tribe's time had finally come to fly up to the Great Mother, board, and go home after centuries of waiting for rescue. It was a moment of frenzy as well as elation. Gray Feather's marriage celebration was quickly abandoned.

Gray Feather took a broom and started to assist in the uncovering of the space craft as did Jack Benson and Ralph Archer his doctor friends from New Jersey. They were seeing a UFO plus uncovering a space ship. In shock, they momentarily got caught up in the moment that never comes to humans. They were interacting with beings from another planet and viewing a UFO coming down the size of ten football fields. It didn't get any better than that when you were a scientist.

After about fifteen minutes of frantic sweeping and clearing of windows, North Star opened the spacecraft's door and started looking for Moon Dance who was the only surviving Pure Weelo who knew how to fly the bullet shaped space flyer. A line of women was formed along with Gray Feather, Ralph Long Legs, and Jack Benson. It was disrespect if you entered before the pilot. She scanned the desert and could not see Moon Dance anywhere.

"Where is Moon Dance?" North Star yelled to the line of women.

"Moon dance . . . "Gray Feather retorted in shock. "What do you mean where is Moon Dance. One of you told me out in the desert that she died two years ago."

All the women looked at each other and then him with big eyes. Each wondered who had told him that lie.

"Moon Dance is alive, Gray Feather." Leaping Lizard stated from her position in the line next to Hissing Cat.

North Star, knowing the time frame for them to fly up to the mother ship was limited, started ushering the women aboard. Last to board would be Hissing Cat, her, and the men. She was sure that Moon Dance would make her way to the space flyer by the time she got everyone aboard. All of the tribe depended on Moon Dance. She had been a scientist and a flight engineer before Noah I crashed. Everyone else in the tribe had held remedial jobs on Noah I. She couldn't wait any longer to get everyone on board. She would take full responsibility for letting everyone board ahead of Moon Dance. Time was of an essence.

When Moon Dance didn't make her way to the spacecraft, North Star stuck her head in the flyer's door and yelled knowing that Pansy Sky Walker was the last to see Moon Dance. "Pansy, where is Moon Dance?"

"I don't know!" Pansy retorted in a catty, snotty voice. She hoped that Moon Dance was gone and out of her life for good. She intended to turn her venom on Hissing Cat now.

Ralph Archer handed Carol Sue, his daughter, into the space craft to one of the women and turned to Gray Feather stating. "I will go look for her."

Ralph knew how much his friend loved Moon Dance and also that his friend had just married someone else thinking Moon Dance was dead. Gray Feather's eyes read pure panic. Turning, Ralph sprinted towards the Hogan in the distance. He knew from Gray Feather's stories that Moon Dance was probably there saying her goodbyes.

Hissing Cat left Gray Feather's side with a smirk grin on her face. She boarded leaving North Star, Jack Benson, and Gray Feather outside of the space craft. She didn't want to have to explain how she had asked the girl who was assisting her to tell Gray Feather that Moon dance was dead. She had done it as a joke. She didn't know that Gray Feather would propose and marry her on the spot out of respect which was the Earth Weelo custom of caring for their old ones. Her joke had turned to her advantage in a big way. She now owned Gray Feather. Only women on Planet Weelo could obtain a divorce. The men had no say so or rights when it came to that. Weelo women owned their men like they were cattle or dogs. Gray Feather could not divorce her or have their marriage annulled for any reason. He was hers. She was delighted.

Within minutes, Ralph was back at the space flyer's door in a state of panic. He whispered into North Star's ear. "Moon dance is dying by the Hogan door. She has let a Rattlesnake bite her. She will not be going with us. She said for all of you to go to hell and take Gray Feather with you because you all have disrespected her."

"Oh God . . . "North Star Whispered to Ralph. "We cannot fly without Moon Dance. She is the only original Weelo that knows how to activate the flight panels. The Weelo men are in Utah. They abandoned us. Hissing Cat is pure Weelo like Moon Dance, but she was a hair dresser on the original Great Mother Ship, Noah

I. She doesn't have a clue as how to activate the flyer. I can fly the space craft, but I cannot activate its flight panels.

"My friend just married an Alien hair dresser?" Ralph asked amused in spite of his panic and wanting to get back to Moon Dance who was dying.

"That is how Hissing Cat has managed to marry human chiefs and hold prominent positions in the tribes down thru the centuries. She has used her cosmetology skills to make herself more attractive than the rest of us women. Moon Dance is the prize. She was a research scientist and flight engineer. She can fly any type of spacecraft the mother Ship has in its bays. " North Star replied. "I was a simple space flyer pilot trainee when the ship crashed."

"Moon Dance is the only old one who can fly this craft?" Ralph asked in shock looking in the door way of the flyer at all the women who were seated and waiting to take off.

"I can fly it, but it takes Moon Dance's eye code to activate it. This was her space craft. Her eye code is like Earth's keys. None of us will be going home if she doesn't look at the flyer's panel and activate it. Hissing Cat has already abandoned her Earth Body. Without boarding the Great Mother, she will cease to be in the Earth's atmosphere within twenty-four hours. The rest of us will be doomed to thousands of years of incarnations till another craft comes for us. The Great Mother waits for no one. Twenty minutes to board is all we have."

Gray Feather heard what Ralph was whispering to North Star and instantly started running for the Hogan. He didn't care if he had married Hissing Cat out of respect. It was Moon Dance he loved and it was her that he had returned to the desert for. She was the other half of his heart and the only woman he would ever love. How could he have made such a rash decision in the desert marrying Hissing Cat?

Ralph left North Star and instantly ran after his friend. Jack Benson wasn't far behind the two of them. The three doctors were friends from New Jersey and did everything together.

North Star stuck her head in the space craft flyer door and bounced a crystal mind beam off of Pansy Skywalker seeing that Pansy had a dark smirk on her face. North Star was a mind reader as well as a planetary pilot trainee. On Weelo, she was the equivalent of your local Palm Reader who had a hobby or passion for flying. Reading Pansy's mind, she knew that their story teller had planned to say nothing and leave their planet's renowned woman scientist, Moon Dance, behind. In reading Pansy's mind, North Star saw Pansy for the vindictive, disrespectful, half human being she was.

"I am pure Weelo, Pansy Sky Walker, and I can read your mind. You have disrespected our medicine woman. If it hadn't been for Moon Dance, the ten or so of us would have ceased to be in the harsh New Mexico desert when the men abandoned us. Moon Dance hunted snakes, fed us, and rocked your child of disrespect because you wouldn't for the last two or so years. I see in your face that you have intended to leave her behind. I will ask the council to imprison you when we board the ship for insubordination. Moon Dance is irreplaceable on our planet. You will not be granted Weelo citizenship nor live as a free Weelo. You will become someone's slave, the punishment for disrespect of an officer. This is Moon Dance's Space flyer that you sit in. I hope I become your master. I will see that you wash her feet with your tears and shine her shoes someday. Furthermore, you will be required to tell Gray Feather of your tricking him into making love to you in the desert. I am Weelo and can read every thought and action that you have ever had. You have kept Gray Feather and Moon Dance apart. You will be denied ever having a mate as punishment. I, North Star, swear it in front of everyone here." She stated and then turned to Hissing Cat. "I also know that it was you that had your girl tell Gray Feather that Moon Dance was dead. You have also disrespected her. You married Gray Feather in deceit. You will have to go before the council also. What they will do, I do not know. I will testify against you."

Pansy jumped up in an effort to get out of the space craft. The women wrestled her and forced her back into her seat. A look of disbelief spread across Hissing Cat's face. She hadn't asked Gray Feather to marry her. He had asked her.

Meanwhile, out in the desert, Moon Dance's human body died. Reaching the burnt out Hogan, breathless from running, Gray Feather fell to his knees seeing Moon Dance limp as a rag doll with her eyes rolled back. She was leaning against the Hogan wall where he had once sat counseling the Weelo tribe with her. He could see that her eyes were set in death. He quickly took her pulse and shook her calling her name. She didn't respond. In tears, he took her in his arms and held her close to him letting their hearts beat as one. Then he felt her human heart beat stop.

"No . . . . !" he yelled realizing there was no hope for her. They were in the middle of the desert in New Mexico. The nearest medical help was a couple hundred miles away. Gray Feather rocked her in his arms bursting into tears. "Only you Moon Dance, I love only you." He wailed.

She didn't hear him because the human body she was traveling in was dead. Her spirit's ears were muffled by the dead human body she was in. She could not hear till she unzipped the human body and discarded it. She assumed it was one of the women of the tribe distraught over her suicide.

Gray Feather's heart shattered into a million pieces because it was her that he truly loved. He cradled her dead body crying and eyeing the empty rattlesnake bag and the bite on her neck. He knew that she had killed herself over him and in the spot where they had spent many happy hours sitting together.

"Please forgive me, Moon Dance. One of the women told me you had died. I married Hissing Cat out of respect. I did not know you were here. I love only you, only you." He wailed rocking back and forth with her dead body in his arms.

In uncontrollable sobbing, he picked her seventy-six year old, hundred pound limp body up to carry her back to the flyer with him. A hand touched him gently on his shoulder. He turned. It was Jack.

"Let me take her, Michael. Hissing Cat will never understand. You are married! I will see that Moon Dance's body is on board. "

"I am a fool! I know who tricked me and told me that Moon Dance was dead. She will pay." Gray Feather stated with tear stained face, red eyes, and angry expression.

"Don't make any rash decisions, Michael. We have all been tricked or fooled at one time or another. Afterward, we walk forward smarter for the experience. There is every possibility that you are going to have an interesting good life with Hissing Cat. You are a doctor, a scientist. Traveling with this alien tribe by space ship to planet Weelo is the chance of a lifetime, a fantasy. Suck it up and do what is right for these women that have accepted you as their chief, even though you are human. You are an Earth scientist going into space and interacting with beings from another planet." Jack Benson stated trying to comfort and encourage his distraught friend, Michael Haven Gray Feather.

Gently, Dr. Michael Haven Gray Feather reluctantly let his friend Jack Benson remove his beloved Moon Dance from his arms.

"Go, Michael, tell them to hold the space craft. I will be there in a moment with her. You have a tribe to lead and a wife to respect. I will care for the woman your heart really belongs to and see that her body makes it on board. Don't think with your heart right now. Sometimes we must sacrifice ourselves for the greater good. That is what you are going to have to do.! Think of yourself as marrying Hissing Cat for the greater good. We make mistakes, but we can turn those mistakes into great accomplishments if we put our head to it."

"I am a fool! Moon Dance must have seen me with Hissing Cat. I have destroyed the other half of my heart. I am a murderer." Gray Feather replied in a broken voice.

Wiping tears on the back of his hand, Gray Feather reluctantly headed back to the space flyer. Jack Benson walked behind carrying a very thin, limp as a rag doll, hundred pound Moon Dance. When Jack Benson neared the space craft with Moon Dance in his arms, he spoke to North Star waiting at the door.

"Moon Dance Sleeps, she is dead." Jack whispered to North Star.

North Star took a look at Moon Dance's human body and then stood on tip toes whispering into Jack's ear, "She is not dead, Doctor Benson. Only her human body is dead. Help me get her to the pilot's seat. I need her eyes to activate the flyer. Look into her eyes. She is staring out at us. She intends to enter another human form to hide from Gray Feather and his disrespect. She just told me so with mind telepathy. She will unzip her human body once we are gone. She does not intend to go home with us. Her heart is shattered. She wants to be left in the desert."

"She what . . .?" Jack Benson asked turning Moon Dance's face toward him and staring into her eyes. He could see a familiar, lost, hurting soul, staring back at him. "Oh shit . . ."

Carrying her gently, he made his way to the cockpit passing all of the women and Michael Haven Gray Feather who had Hissing Cat hanging on his arm grinning. There, he gently sat her dead human body in an upright position in the pilot's seat. North Star turned Moon Dance's face toward the flight panel controls. The panels did not activate.

"Something is wrong!" North Star whispered to Jack Benson turning Moon Dance's face toward her and staring into her eyes.

As Jack Benson was reaching to pull curtains between the cockpit and the passenger area to give him, North Star, and Moon Dance privacy; he could see Gray Feather about to lose it. His face was ashen. Jack closed the curtains preventing the women and Gray Feather from seeing what was going on.

"She has purposely killed her human body and will look for a new baby conception to enter far away from her pain of loving Gray Feather." North Star whispered to Jack Benson. "In a new baby, she will not remember herself as Moon Dance or as having ever loved a man named Gray Feather. She is in a nightmare state needing to forget Gray Feather. Marrying Hissing Cat was his ultimate and final betrayal of her. She refuses to activate her space craft panels. She just told me to tell all of her disrespectful tribe, including me, to go to Hell! I ran also to the spring to greet and welcome back Gray Feather. I admit my guilt."

"Oh crap. I know what Michael did that she is angry about. Why in the Hell would all of you being pure Weelo disrespect Moon Dance? Gray Feather is human." He muttered. "Damn it . . . Don't any of you have any loyalty? Do you all know who this woman named Moon Dance is?"

"I know, but the others seem to have forgotten and are ungrateful for her sacrifices on Earth to see that they all have survived. A third of the women in there have crushes on Gray Feather. He was a good man and good to all of us when he was here before as our medicine man. We all loved him."

"I am Weelo like you, North Star and have been making my way back to this tribe for centuries. I was the doctor on the Great Mother Ship and Moon Dance was untouchable by me. She was a brilliant Scientist and Flight Engineer. There is not a woman on this craft that is fit to kiss her feet much less sit in the seats of her spacecraft. The Great Mother Ship has returned for her, not all of you. God forbid she should ever haul all of you into Weelo court for disrespect of a flight officer. She could see all of you demoted to street sweepers or toilet cleaners if not worse."

"I am guilty. I admit my guilt. However, I want to go home and so do all of the others. Help me get Moon Dance to focus her Weelo eyes on her control panel. Only she can activate this space craft. I cannot activate it. I was just a pilot trainee when the Great Mother Ship crashed. However, I think I can fly it and get us to the mother ship. Moon Dance keeps closing her Weelo eyes like she is refusing to activate her flyer. We will all perish if she doesn't help us this one last time. Surely, you want to go home." North Star stated with tears in her eyes.

Jack Benson stepped to Moon Dance's side and turned her dead human face towards him. He stared into her Weelo eyes and tried to say with his mind how much he respected her, remembered her, and wanted to get to know her. He told her that he had cracked his crystal skull when the Great Mother Ship crashed and had lost most of his ability to communicate telepathically. Then he turned her face to North Star.

"I need you to ask her if she heard my mind words."

North Star stared into Moon Dance's Weelo eyes that were looking out of the dead human body.

"She says she heard about every third word you thought. She also said she wants to be taken back off the ship so she can exit her human body without Gray Feather seeing. She said she is thru with all of us and refuses to activate the control panels. She plans to abandon all of us and let us fend for ourselves just as we all abandoned her."

"Tell her quickly that I have not abandoned her or disrespected her. Tell her that I have been making my way to her. Tell her that I will carry her off the plane and stay on Earth with her if she will activate the panels and let all of you go home. Tell her . . . tell her I was in love with her on The Great Mother Ship but never got a chance to approach her. Tell her that I know she is the prize, not Hissing Cat the hair dresser or Pansy the half breed. Tell her that Gray Feather is a fool, but I am not. I know what a brilliant scientist and flight engineer she is and that it would be the greatest of honor to have her on my arm. I am not interested in hair dressers or half breeds."

North Star stared into Moon Dance's eyes and conveyed the message telepathically. Moon Dance still closed her eyes when North Star turned her face toward the control panel.

"We must hurry and get thru to her. The Great Mother Ship is above us and on a time schedule. She is purposely closing her eyes on the panel. Help me Jack Benson. We will all perish without her." North Star replied in a panic. Hissing Cat has already left her body. If we do not fly, she will die within hours."

Jack Benson once more turned Moon Dance's face to him and stared into her eyes. Then he tried to think the words "I love you and I want you!" three times and send them to her with his thoughts in hopes she heard one of them. He was pleased with his attempt. There was a sparkle that suddenly flashed from her eyes.

Once more, North Star stared into Moon Dance's eyes.

"She says she is in a dark place of the Weelo heart and that she needs time to heal. She says that she will consider your words and give you an answer when she is not thinking with pain."

Jack Benson grinned and turned Moon Dance's face to him and stared into her eyes. "I will share your dark place of the heart and make it better for you. I am a doctor and also a very lonely man. I need you."

Jack Benson had fallen in love with her thousands of years before on the Great Mother Ship, Noah I. He knew he was still in love with the eyes and the woman scientist that was hiding in the dead human body seated at the pilot's control panel.

"I will wait for your dark heart to sing again." He repeated in thought three times staring into her eyes." Activate the panel, Moon Dance. Do what is right for your Weelo tribe just once more. I will carry your human body off this plane once you do and remain on Earth with you. You can trust me. I have no reason to lie to you. I am Weelo and a man of respect."

North Star turned Moon Dance's face and eyes towards the control panels once more. After a moment, the panel dash lit up like a Christmas tree and strange humming sounds emitted from the panels. It seemed that North Star understood what the hums were. She took the co- pilot's seat and manned the controls pushing buttons here and there. Then she looked up at Jack and whispered.

"Gray Feather will remember her as the human body she wears. He will not recognize her when she returns home someday in Weelo form. She says she has no friends in this tribe and that all have betrayed her, even me. I am guilty. I went to meet Gray Feather in the desert disrespecting her. Gray Feather did abandon us. She wishes you to slip her human body out the pilot's door and leave her behind in the desert. She says she will unzip her human mask, her human body, and enter a new human life as soon as we are gone. She says for you to go ahead and go home to Weelo with the others. She thanks you for your kind words and she won't forget them."

Jack stared into Moon Dance's eyes and he could read loneliness and a broken woman there.

"Open the door and let me slip out with her. I will not be going with you, North Star. I will stay with Moon Dance and we will be a tribe of two. I will step and reincarnate along with her till another rescue ship is sent for us."

North Star rose from her co-pilot's seat and opened the small space craft door that was next to her pilot seat. She then stared once more into moon Dance's eyes thinking. "I am sorry, Moon Dance. I did indeed run to the desert to greet Gray Feather. Forgive me! My allegiance should have been to you knowing he betrayed you a pure Weelo like me with the half breed Pansy Skywalker. I will see that your enemies pay for their disrespect when we reach Weelo. I swear my allegiance to you, knowing you have activated the spacecraft for us. We all deserve to die in the desert. I will not forget who made it possible for me to go home. I will name my first child after you someday."

Jack Benson picked up Moon Dance's body and quietly exited the space craft using the tiny door next to the co-pilot's seat. Those beyond the closed curtains, including Gray Feather, did not know that jack Benson and Moon Dance were not on board as the space craft started to lift from the desert floor.

Standing with Moon dance's body in his arms, Jack Benson watched Moon Dance's bullet shaped space craft rise about twenty five feet into the air and then fly upward in a circling pattern. Placing the dead human body of Moon Dance gently on the desert sand, he stood shading his eyes with one hand watching the phenomena. The space craft, with his friends Doctor Michael Haven Gray Feather and Doctor Ralph Archer on board, disappeared into the open dock of the great Mother Ship. Then, like a flash of lightning, The Great Mother Ship, Noah II, shot off into the universe and was gone.

CHAPTER THREE

HOVERING IN SPIRIT FORM

Jack Benson was standing staring into the sky when Moon Dance broke from her human body in Spirit form and stepped up next to him in a body that was similar to that of Hissing Cat. She had blue skin and seemed to float in a filmy blue ghost like form. Feeling her presence, Jack turned to look at her and his heart jumped into his throat. She was gorgeous just as she had been thousands of years before when she was the renowned Scientist on board the Great Mother Ship Noah I and he was the ship's medical doctor. Just as North Star had said, Hissing Cat was a dog next to Moon Dance. There was a gentle naturalness in Moon Dance's beauty that he just wanted to get lost in, if ever he was given the opportunity. She was the woman of his dreams. On Earth men's scale of one to ten, ten did not describe her beauty. She was more like a hundred and ten.

"I must go." She stated standing next to him. "I have twenty four hours of Earth time to find a new human body to enter and live. Do you wish to step from the body you are in or do you wish to return to New Jersey and live out your current human existence?"

"I have chosen to accompany you, Moon Dance. I will go where you go. Your people will be my people. I will be faithful to you and help you build a new tribe of Weelo." Jack Benson stated eyeing her beauty. He felt like a teenager with butterflies in his stomach. She was breath taking.

"I am honored, Jack Benson, that you have chosen to travel with me. I once longed and dreamed to go home to planet Weelo. Now, I do not wish to return to Weelo for reasons of the heart. I am honored that such a great Weelo, as well as doctor, would consider staying behind with me. May I ask why? I no longer believe in love. It is just a word that now means nightmare to me."

"I have done incarnation after reincarnation as a single doctor. I have never taken the time for a relationship. Human women are dense in their thinking compared to Weelo women. I want to mate with a pure Weelo, not a human. Work down thru the centuries has not been a pleasant companion in the night. My repeated life on Earth as Dr. Jack Benson has been very lonely. I need you Moon Dance. We are both Weelo. I know that we could spend a marvelous Eternity together. I am willing to wait for you to get over Gray Feather. Time heals."

"Love hurts, Jack Benson. You and I are not going there. Love scars the Weelo soul and it is not pleasant to deal with. If I could go back, I would have let a rattlesnake bite me the day before Gray Feather arrived on the reservation. He is a scar that hurts and will never go away. It would have been better for me, as a Weelo, had I not met him. I knew better than to let myself fall in love with a human. I was an old fool. You have been smarter than me in that category."

"If it had not been for Michael, I would not have found my way home to you and the other Weelo. I do not regret knowing him." Jack Benson stated looking at his human body. "Help me exit this human body. Do I unzip from the bottom or the head? I have forgotten some things due to the crack in my crystal skull. Sometimes, the instructional part of my Weelo crystal skull doesn't work since the crash. I am a bit cloudy on some things."

"Well, in case you are currently in a cloud mode, after twenty four hours on Earth without a body to enter, you and I will cease to be. We must find new human bodies to host us. On planet Weelo we are eternal and live forever. On Earth, however, we are susceptible to death or ceasing to be when we discard our human bodies. We need the warmth of the bodies to survive."

"I suppose we are probably going to have to choose human adult bodies, aren't we. We haven't had time to plan tribal pregnancies to enter."

"I am afraid so, Jack Benson. At least we won't have to put up with Hissing Cat and Gray Feather seeing us in less than desirable human bodies. We cannot be picky tonight."

"Hissing Cat and Gray Feather are married and Weelo marriages are forever and Eternity. Somehow, Moon Dance, you must not judge your life by how he might see you. It no longer matters how he sees you. He is married. Don't let him own you when he has no right to do so. He has made a permanent choice. He has a wife."

"You are right, Jack Benson. However, in my nightmare Gray Feather has two wives, not one. He gave Pansy Skywalker a child before returning to New Jersey. He is married to her also. Weelo law says if you give a child to a woman, you are married to her and she owns you. Hissing Cat is Gray Feather's second wife. I will not be his third or his mistress. Pansy Sky Walker rubbed his child in my face for years after he left us. I will not play second fiddle to either of Gray Feather's two wives. I regret ever loving him. I regret even more that I am not capable of loving you. I made a bad choice and I am paying dearly for it."

"One day your heart will sing again. I will go where you go and wait for your heart to discover me." Jack Benson stated looking into her eyes.

"The ship is gone and now it is time for us to face our future and our current need for a body to incarnate in." Moon Dance stated stepping in front of Jack Benson. "I will unzip your body, but it will be up to you to find a new body with in twenty-four hours to enter. It is rare that two infants are conceived in one area. I will say goodbye for now. I plan to journey to the nearest town and enter a new pregnancy if I can find one. You must do the same. We will find our way to each other again. Perhaps my next human heart will not be affected by my Weelo one that is shut down."

"You and I are meant to be together, Moon Dance. In spite of my cracked crystal skull, I remember being the Doctor on the Great Mother Ship, Noah I, and the great crush I had on you back then. On the Great Mother Ship, I couldn't get past all of the influential Weelo male bees buzzing around you to get you to notice me. Now is my chance."

"I am sorry I didn't pay you any attention back on the Great Mother Ship. I was indeed plagued by bees carrying bouquets of flowers." She replied suddenly grinning and trying to remember him from the ship.

"Are you sure that Gray Feather is the other half of your heart? I want to be!"

"Your question I cannot answer. I feel that I am no longer a Weelo woman capable of love. I am shattered. Crustal hearts are like crystal skulls. They break."

"I understand and I am willing to wait for your crystal heart to heal and love again."

"I must go, Benson." Moon Dance stated. She then took his hand in hers, raised it up to his face, and pointed his index finger to the center of his head and then drew a line with it down his human body. Immediately, his human body slit open. Stepping from his body, he too had blue skin, three eyes, crystal ears, and raven black hair. He was also a blue, filmy, ghost like form. He looked at Moon Dance, smiled, and placed his filmy blue hand on her cheek in a loving gesture.

"Eternity, Moon Dance, Eternity." He stated looking her directly in her eyes. Then he kissed her on the cheek.

"Go, Jack Benson. Find a human body to enter and I will draw you to me. Listen for the sound of shattering crystal and the whistle of my human lips. My crystal heart shatters over and over making a breaking sound. I cannot stop it. When I think of Gray Feather, my crystal heart breaks all over again. The two sounds are how you will know me."

Like the flash of a night star's ray, they shot off separately into the sky seeking new human forms to enter and live human lives once more.

In the desert of New Mexico, two human bodies were left to the elements to rot and decompose. The two human bodies known as Doctor Jack Benson and the Weelo medicine woman named Moon Dance would be skeletons before the week was out and animals would scatter their human bones.

CHAPTER FOUR

MOON DANCE LIVES AGAIN

Moon Dance, in filmy blue spirit form, shot down to the edge of the Rio Grande and started following it west till she floated across the New Mexico state line into Arizona. She followed the river till she spotted a town with a hospital on the northern side of the Rio. There she shot thru a glass window without breaking it and started looking for a new body to live in. She preferred a new conception to enter, but she would settle for an adult body if she had to, one that a human soul had left. She was surprised to find that the hospital's OBGYN floors were shut down for remodeling. The nursery as well as pediatrics was closed. There would be no new conception or discarded dead human baby's body that she could enter. She realized that she didn't have time to look for a new hospital. Making a quick decision, she would float down to surgery and ICU to see if there was a dead body possibility there. She knew humans got old, died, had accidents, and were subject to terminal illnesses. She floated into the surgery unit to look around.

Moon Dance hovered over a body that lay on an operating table. A young woman about the age of twenty- two was being operated on for what looked like a bad heart. She watched as the surgery monitors all went off and the girl on the operating table stopped breathing. Then the twentyish girl rose from her body in spirit form and hovered near the ceiling with Moon Dance.

"Are you going to return to your body?" Moon Dance asked pointing downward at doctors and nurses trying frantically to revive the girl's human body doing CPR.

"No, I have lived out my mission here. This is my predestined exit point. I will cross over and go home as soon as my tunnel of light or light port appears. I am a scientist from Plutonia. I was doing an incarnation on Earth studying the human heart. The girl down there died of heart failure when she was six. I have been using her body since for scientific research. On Plutonia, we are trying to decide whether human hearts can survive our atmosphere. We need new blood in our species. Our population has almost quit reproducing. We are considering taking breeding stock from Planet Earth to increase our population. We are down to about four hundred thousand beings and have had only ten conceptions in the last five years. My study of the girl's human body below and its heart is completed. Now, I must go home and report my findings."

"So you are a citizen of one of the seven moons of Planet Weelo." Moon Dance stated.

"Yes, I am going home this evening by light port." The female spirit stated who had a purple, misty, ghost like spirit form with long white hair. Weelo had blue skin and raven colored hair.

"Would you have any objections if I borrowed your female human body down there for a few years instead of letting it die? The human body I was traveling in died of a Rattlesnake bite this morning. I am not ready to return to Planet Weelo yet and I am looking for a new body to travel in for awhile."

"I should have known from your blue skin that you are from Weelo? Several years ago, I visited there with my plutonian parents who were attending a science conference. I gather that your population is also suffering from a lack of births. Are you a doctor or scientist also?"

"I was a research scientist on the Great Mother Ship, Noah I, before it crashed on Earth. I was harvesting Earth animals and plants to study. Since then, I have been stepping from body to body down thru the centuries waiting for a rescue ship along with about a hundred scattered surviving Weelo."

"That is a bummer, as the humans say. One human incarnation has been enough for me. You can share my light port and go home if you wish. I could then fly you home from Plutonia in my brand new red space flyer that I have been itching to try out on a little road trip as the humans say."

"Thanks for the offer, but I am purposely staying here. The Great Mother Ship actually came for me earlier in the day. I sent my tribe home to Weelo, but I remained here for reasons I don't wish to go into. I am going to do a few more incarnations on Earth."

For a brief moment, the two spirits watched the nurses and doctors below still working frantically on the female human body.

"I have no further use of the body. I am a scientist and if you can use the body for your own information gathering; that is okay with me."

"Thank you. I won't forget this. When I return to Weelo, I will repay you somehow. Perhaps we could share a few days on the blue beaches of Weelo and stay overnight in a Bed and Breakfast at my expense."

"You are on." The Plutonian female stated grinning. "Let me tell you quickly about my life as the girl below. She is named Sleeping Moon. Her father is dead and her mother disappeared in the desert a few years ago and hasn't been found. No one knows what happened to her except me. She was harvested for my planet and sent by light port to be studied as a reproduction specimen. She was what the humans call a fertile Myrtle. The girl has two brothers, White Eagle and Night Hawk, who are wealthy cattle ranchers. I am not especially fond of the family's cook, Charlie Elkhorn. I will let you find out on your own why. The girl lives with a crazy grandmother named Song Bird. If in doubt as what to talk about till you fit in and learn them as individuals, claim you can't remember due to your surgery. A week of living with those yahoos and you will be ready to half kill them. They are crazier than bed bugs. I definitely do not want to return to them. Death down there was Heaven. The girl's human body was plagued with pains and health complications. If I were you, I would choose another human body. You are going to hate the girl's family." She grinned biting her spirit lip.

"I do not have a choice. I am running out of time to incarnate." Moon dance replied.

"My human family, down there, thinks out of the box to see what mischief and craziness that they can get into. I give you thirty days and you will be looking for another body to enter."

"I need a body now and I will deal with your Earth human family. Surviving centuries of mad humans and their pettiness has hardened me. I am no wimp!"

"What are you going to do about the girl's bad heart? It is not repairable by those less intelligent human doctors below."

"I will repair it. Weelo are experienced in the repair of human hearts. We experimented thousands of years ago on animals we harvested here. It is a grade school experience for us. The heart repair will not be a problem for me." Moon Dance stated thinking she wished she could heal her emotional heart as easy.

"I have got to go. Here comes my light port." The Plutonian female stated. A shaft of light entered the room and she floated into it.

When the female spirit of the scientist from Plutonia was gone, Moon Dance floated down to the body that had its chest open and entered it as a spirit. She lay down in it trying it on for size. Then she caused the human heart to start beating.

"Doctor . . . "yelled a nurse who was covering the dead human body with a sheet. "She is breathing!"

Excited, the doctor and his assistants returned to the table and started frantically working on her. They had stopped trying to revive her two minutes before. They were shocked when her body jolted and she took a gasping breath with the oxygen tube flying from her nose. They had never witnessed a corpse coming back to life again on its own. Sleeping Moon had been deceased and pronounced so.

CHAPTER FIVE

JEROME'S LIFE ALTERING EXPERIENCE

Jack Benson, having abandoned his human body known as Doctor Jack Benson, flashed across the hours of twilight looking for a body to enter. In Weelo spirit form, he was making his way toward Tucson, Arizona. He felt that a major hospital might be the best place for him to find a body being conceived or discarded in death. Flashing across the sky, he spotted a ranch house facing the Rio Grande on the United States side with all of its lights on. He could also see the flashing of ambulance lights and law enforcement vehicles. He swished down in spirit form to check it out. The front door of the hacienda type ranch home stood wide open. A distraught older man stood on the front walkway speaking with a sheriff's department officer and ambulance EMTs. Jack floated down and listened to the conversation going on. He didn't feel in any particular rush. He had twenty-four hours to find another body and he was enjoying the freedom of being able to travel and fly in spirit form. He had spent his last lifetime in a stuffy office with his nose in books and in psychiatrist case load files. He was ready for some freedom and change. His two friends were headed for Planet Weelo, so he had nothing to go back to New Jersey for.

"I am sorry, John. We tried. Your son took a lethal dose of sleepers. He was gone before we arrived and started to work on him. We can keep performing CPR, but it is too late. The pills have had a couple of hours to work." The county Deputy sheriff stated removing his hat. Apparently, he knew the older rancher.

"Why do you think he did it?" the older man named John asked with tears welling up in his eyes.

"According to your housekeeper, he wanted to move back to California and the gay lifestyle he had there. He was afraid to tell you." The deputy replied not going into details.

"Bull shit . . . !" A misty gray female form stated floating up and hovering by Jack Benson. "I took the pills because my male lover dumped me for a cross dresser in Las Vegas. I didn't see it coming and I couldn't deal with it. I was very high strung; you know, overly emotional living in that awful man's body." The Female form stated striking up a conversation with Jack Benson.

Jack Benson looked at the misty female form and then down at the male form she had exited. "Don't you want to return to your body and give it another try?" He asked knowing that he was witnessing the death of a homosexual man.

"Hell no, I intend to stay Earth bound as a ghost and haunt the pee wad out of my lover who dumped me tonight for a dog walker named Georgie. My lover Harley dumped me for a poodle boy who is on food stamps. I have money, or did have."

"What about the older man down there that is distraught over you. Don't you want to return to your body for him?"

"That is my dad, John Mason. He owns the ranch below and has always been ashamed of me because of my feminine ways. I was a homosexual who wanted to be a seamstress and own a fabric store, not play nursemaid to long horn crapping steers. I am definitely not a rancher and do not want to return to that male body and the life that goes with it. I am a girl, in case you have not noticed."

"What is your name? My name is Jack Benson and I am a Weelo looking for a body to incarnate in."

"I love your name, Jack Benson. Jerome Mason was my name down there. However, I am a girl spirit and prefer to be called Jeri Ann Jerome Mason much to my red necked father's displeasure. I lived in that dreadful male body down there. My father never understood that he had a daughter, not a son."

"I am pleased to meet you, Jeri Ann. How old is your discarded male body down there?"

"That fool of a male body down there was born on the fourth of July twenty five years ago. My mother who is deceased used to call me her little fire cracker. My dad however, has always seen me as a sissy sparkler."

"How would you feel if I should enter your dead body and live out your life as your father's son? I need stability while I search for the medicine woman of my tribe called Moon Dance. I want to incarnate and make my way to her. We both died in the desert about twelve or so hours ago. I love her and must make my way back to her."

"How sweet . . ." Jerome stated in a feminine voice. "Was she really cute, cuter than me?"

"You are one damn good looking female spirit, Jeri Ann Jerome, but Moon Dance gives me butterflies and goose bumps looking at her."

"You are a romantic, I can tell!" Jeri Ann stated flirting with him. "If she is dead, I think I could cause you to have a butterfly or two. Are you interested?"

"Moon Dance's old human body is dead, but her Weelo Spirit is looking for a body to enter just like me. However, should she ever turn me down for any reason, I would be open to pursuing a possible relationship with you. I like sticky voiced females."

"You are one sweet thing, Jack Benson. I think you just might convince me to forget my lover Harley the cross dresser. You are giving me goose bumps."

"For now, Jeri Ann, I am not available. But, you never know."

"The thought of you in my body down there is delicious, Jack Benson." Jeri Ann Jerome stated batting her eyes in a serious flirtatious manner."Harley, the cross dresser, can go fly a kite. I think I have just fallen in love with you. I have never been with a man who had blue skin. I like what I see."

"I like what I see too, Jeri Ann. However, I must try to make a go of it with Moon Dance first."

"Will you be living down along the Rio, Jack Benson?" She questioned making her voice drip with syrup.

"Yes, I plan to meet Moon Dance somewhere below along the Rio."

"Tell Moon Dance for me to move over. I think I will give it another shot down there and make my way to you. I am going to give your Moon Dance a little competition and I always get my man."

"I will tell Moon Dance." Jack Benson replied grinning.

"You have given me a new lease on life, Jack Benson. I will live to meet you down there somewhere. You are my new man and Moon Dance can take a hike. You suit me."

"You mean you aren't going to let me enter and travel a while in your body down there?"

"Nope, I am turning over a new leaf. I will fly back down there, resume my life, make my father proud of me, and keep an eye out for you down by the Rio. When you least expect it, I will sweep into your life. I am the one for you."

"I have got to go, Jeri Ann Jerome. Since you will not let me have the body below, I must find a body somewhere to host me. Till we meet again, may our paths always wind their way back to each other."

"We are friends for now, Jack Benson. However, I will be your lover in the future. The cross dresser in Vegas was just a set up by the universe to help me make my way to you. What do you do for a living?" Jeri Ann Jerome Mason asked as an afterthought.

"I always reincarnate and become a doctor on Earth." He replied eyeing the misty form of a girl he actually found quite amusing. She definitely was not the most brilliant woman he had ever met, but he found her fascinating. It was something about her squeal and sticky voice. It excited him.

Jeri Ann squealed with delight. "Every girl wants to marry a doctor. I am no different. My mother would be so . . . proud of me if she were alive. I can just see you and me someday as Doctor and Mrs. Jeri Ann Jack Benson. Do you make a lot of money? I have expensive taste when it comes to shoes and handbags."

"I am comfortable or was. The woman I choose to be with will be well taken care of." Jack Benson replied grinning.

"Ooh . . ." squealed Jeri Ann Jerome once more. "I want a man who can take care of me. You are definitely the one, Jack Benson. Don't you go fooling around with anyone but Moon Dance! I am going to let you have a little fling with her so that you can get her out of your system. Other than her, you watch yourself or I just might cut off your yang. Do you get my meaning?"

"I get your point, Jeri Ann Jerome. Tell me a little about yourself so I will have something to think about till the next time we meet."

"I graduated high school in Phoenix and went to Berkley in California. I dropped out of the university and entered cosmetology school and became a hair dresser."

Jack bit his lip and snorted not meaning to interrupt her. His friend Michael Haven Gray Feather had just married a hair dresser. Was there something going around? He now had a hairdresser hitting on him. Granted he, Ralph, and Michael always did things together, but this was ridiculous.

"Don't you laugh at me being a hair dresser, Jackie-poo! One day you will need my services to help hide your balding spot that is on the way to happening."

Jack slapped his hand on the top of his head, "It is showing?" He asked vainly wondering if Moon Dance had seen it.

"Only I could love that spot and kiss it every night, Jackie-poo." Jeri Ann Jerome returned in her sticky voice that was drawing him in. She then continued, "I returned home for the funeral of my mother which was a big mistake. I should have just grieved my way and stayed where I belonged. My father talked me into staying here on the ranch, which was a bad mistake. In California, I designed and

33

made all of my own clothes, made a mean casserole of enchiladas, and spent weekends in Las Vegas with Harley, my former cross dresser lover. My favorite color is pink and now my favorite male is you."Jeri Ann Jerome giggled while batting her Spirit Being eyes at him once more.

"I want you to do two things for me till I return. One, I want you to forget yourself for once and get to know your father. His tears down there are real and he is heartbroken over losing you. Give him a chance to get to know you. Tell him you are a girl in a male body. Two, if Moon Dance should cross your path, befriend her for me. She has no family or friends. She could really use a girl friend like you. Plus, I just might marry the both of you. One could have my heart and the other my yang."

"You are a naughty boy! " Jeri Ann Jerome giggled and then added. "I have dibs on the yang."

"I must go now, Jeri Ann Jerome Mason. I have got to find a host body. May my deceased Jewish mother be your guardian angel and watch over you till we meet again." Jack Benson stated reaching out and hugging her.

"Oh Jack Benson, you are making me cry. Get out of here." Jeri Ann Jerome said taking one filmy hand and fanning her spirit eyes that were filling with tears."

"Just so you don't forget me, I have a parting Jewish gift for you."Jack Benson stated. He took Jeri Ann Jerome in his arms and kissed her like there was no tomorrow, a kiss that she would never forget. Then he released her laughing and shot off into the night sky.

Jerome Jeri Ann watched him go and waved with tears trickling down her filmy spirit form face. She had just had a life altering experience. She had fallen in love with a straight arrow Jewish man and he had kissed her. It didn't get any better than that.

When Jack Benson was out of sight, Jeri Ann in mist form floated down and reentered her human form, a wimpy little male named Jerome. She wiggled about till she was comfortable and then started the human body's heart. Needless to say, the paramedics were shocked by their corpse covered with a sheet suddenly starting to wiggle, breathe, and cough. They quickly uncovered Jerome Mason and started new measures to save him. In ten minutes time, Jerome Mason was sitting up on the side of his bed, vomiting the residue of pills, and violently puking up what was left of a supper of undigested enchiladas and beans. The contents of his stomach were grossing the paramedics out. Undigested enchiladas and beans is not a pretty sight nor does it smell good.

Defying the paramedics, Jeri Ann Jerome refused to be transported to the hospital. He got up and headed for his shower to clean up and shampoo his hair. He had a new lease on life and a new love to dream about.

In total shock, his father followed him to the shower.

"Jerome, you should really let the paramedics take you to the hospital and check you out. You were dead. I said my good- byes to you. It is a miracle that you are alive."

"My sweet, sweet Daddy . . . I know I was dead. I have been to the afterlife and returned with a new lease on life. I am going to live every minute now to the fullest and that includes fishing, camping, and hunting with you. I met my soul mate while I was on the other side flying above this house. His name is Jack Benson and he is a psychiatrist. Mother would be so proud of me. I am going to marry a Jewish doctor. He said I could have his yang." Jeri Ann Jerome giggled and squealed with delight while pulling off his puked on clothing. He stepped naked into the shower. "You won't even have to pay for the wedding dad. He is comfortable and will buy me all of the shoes and handbags I want. "

"What?" His father gasped in a total state of confusion as to what his son was speaking of.

"I am a girl spirit that just happens to be traveling in this male body. I am your daughter, dad. My soul mate is a psychiatrist and he told me to be nice to you. I will do anything for him including going fishing and hunting with you. I am compromising even though I am a vegetarian."

"Where did you say you met this psychiatrist?"

"I met him after I died and left my body. Oh, there is one thing I want you to do for me. I would like to have a pink gun cabinet put where my sewing machine now sits and hang one of those fishing rod rack thingies above my bed. I am your new girl buddy. I saw your tears when I was floating above you. You love me! Jack pointed that out to me. You don't know how good that makes me feel."

"I have always loved you Jerome. What do you mean you were floating above eyeing my tears?"

"Doctor Jack Benson and I floated about twenty feet off the ground and he kissed me up there, dad. It was wonderful. He made my spirit toes curl up. I have never been so happy in all of my life." Jeri Ann Jerome stated excitedly as he showered.

"Oh shit." John Mason muttered quietly so that Jerome couldn't hear. "He has had some sort of mental collapse and an out of body experience to go with it like they talk about on TV talk shows. I will sign him up for a psychiatric evaluation the first thing in the morning. Just make it thru the night with him, John."

Jeri Ann Jerome stuck his head out of the shower.

"Don't worry about me dad. The affair between me and the cross dresser in Las Vegas is over. It was his breaking up with me that sent me over the edge. It was a destined thing. I can see that now. I would never have met Jack if it hadn't been for my pill popping suicide. I have crossed over and returned to tell about it as they say."

"If you don't mind, Jerome, I think I will sleep here in your room tonight. I'll grab my sleeping bag and you can tell me all about your Jack. I just want to make sure you are okay till morning. You might need me."

"There is no need, dad. I am fine. You wouldn't have a fifth of whiskey around anywhere would you. I have got to cut that nasty enchilada and beans taste out of my mouth with something."

"Jerome, you never drink anything but Light Beer."

"This is a definite whiskey night. Have one with me! Would you like to play some poker? I am going to do anything you want from here on out. Jack Benson asked me to. He is the most wonderful guy dad, even if I have to be one of his two wives. At least I get the better part of him, his yang. Moon Dance can have his heart. Hearts are fickle."

"I don't know what this suicide attempt has done to you, but be sure of one thing Jerome. I love you and I don't want you to ever try it again. If I caused you attempt somehow, I want you to be honest with me and tell me what I have done. I will do my best to make it right with you."

"Don't worry dad. My taking the pills had nothing to do with you. I was having an affair with a cross dresser in Las Vegas. It was his breaking up with me yesterday that I was upset about. Would you mind calling me Jeri Ann? "

"Jeri Ann . . . Jerome . . . I am willing to change. Just don't ever leave me again."

"I am not going anywhere. I have decided to get a waitress job in town and make you proud of me. No more hand outs for me. I don't want any more of your money, dad. I am going to be a working girl and wait for Jack Benson to return to me. "

"But Jeri Ann, you don't have to work. We own the café in town and just about every other business there. We are the wealthiest ranchers in the valley. People come to us to borrow money."

"Don't tell Jack Benson, Dad. I want him buying my handbags and shoes. He's my man."Jeri Ann Jerome stated sticking his head out of the shower. "Turn your back dad. I am a grown girl for Christ's sake. I am not five and you are checking to make sure I shampoo my hair."

"Oh . . . I wasn't thinking Jeri Ann." John Mason replied grinning. He then turned his back.

CHAPTER SIX

SNAKE FOR DINNER

Two months passed. Moon Dance, who had incarnated in the dead human body of a girl named Sleeping Moon, had returned to the family ranch with her new Grandmother Song Bird and her two wealthy cattle rancher brothers named White Eagle and Night Hawk. It was now her second day home. The first day she had wandered about the ranch house and the ranch trying to get her bearings. An infant would adjust, grow, and learn right along with the family it was raised in. She was winging it, trying to fit it, and pump everyone secretly for information about herself. Living with strangers and pretending to know them was nerve wrecking for fear of doing or saying something wrong.

Today, she decided to surprise her new family and provide the meat for dinner. She had gone in search of a Rattlesnake which had been the main source of food when she lived in the New Mexico desert with her former Weelo tribe. She had found a nice one with eight buttons on the tail and was confident that he was going to make a fine dinner for her new family. Moon Dance, now Sleeping Moon, was sure that her two new rancher brothers would give her some respect seeing she was able to do her part in providing for the family. Being treated like an invalid was demeaning to her. She was ready to get on with her new life and be a contributor to the family's needs.

Sleeping Moon looked at the wiggling, hissing, curling snake that she was holding. She held it firmly behind its head and was extremely pleased with herself. However, she was having trouble with her new body she had incarnated in. It didn't move as fast as her old one. It was weak and hadn't been trained to move swiftly. The snake had almost bit her before she managed to get her new body's hand around the snake's neck. She was going to have to exercise this new body and get it in shape.

Suddenly, she realized she did not have her burlap bag from her last life in the New Mexico desert. She had to find a place to store the live snake till dinner. She was considering using her pillowcase temporarily. She hadn't thought about a sack for the snake till she had already caught it. Holding the snake out from her with one hand, she opened the kitchen door of the ranch house and stepped into the hacienda type kitchen leaving the door open. She then stepped to the center of the room intending to head down a hall off the kitchen to her bedroom with intent to put the snake in her pillowcase.

Sleeping Moon's brother, White Eagle, suddenly stepped into the kitchen area from a large side pantry where a freezer was kept. He had just returned from the processing plant with a wild boar that had been sent there to be butchered and processed. Having heard the kitchen door open, he thought it was his brother with the other box of meat from the back of their pickup. He had stepped out from the pantry to see if he needed some help, since both boxes had held seventy five pounds of meat. Seeing Sleeping Moon holding a live Rattlesnake by the neck in their kitchen, he froze in pure fright with his mouth falling open.

"Don't move Sleeping Moon! "He demanded with all of the blood draining from his face. "Why are you holding a live Rattlesnake by the neck?"

Fear gripped White Eagle. He eased toward the kitchen counter where there was a rack of knives. Sleeping Moon, his sister, had just got out of the hospital and rehab after almost dying from open heart surgery. She was weak, frail, and in the eyes of her two brothers needed to be in bed with a nurse watching over her. Was she crazy too? He was in an unexpected panic.

In a flash of memory, White Eagle remembered the years of life and death situations his sister had endured with multiple heart problems and various other related ailments. She had been so fragile as a child that she had been homeschooled. Just the ride in an auto to school was too much stress for her heart. His sister had been pampered, home schooled, spoiled, and watched over very carefully. She was like a breakable China Doll that the whole family had gone out of their way to protect. Now, here she stood with a live rattlesnake in her hand.

White Eagle, with perspiration suddenly breaking out on his forehead, muttered to himself. "Kill the snake and then call the doctor to see if she needs some sort of anti-picking up snake drug."

"What's wrong?" Sleeping Moon asked turning around with the live snake in her hand lifting her arms up and down in excitement. She then scanned the floor beneath her feet in fear of stepping barefoot on a tarantula or scorpion. The girl's shoes in the closet weren't comfortable and she couldn't find a pair of moccasins anywhere. She had resigned herself to going barefoot till she could get the hide of something to make a suitable pair of shoes. She was not in to spike heels and city shoes.

"Stand still . . ." White Eagle once more yelled in sheer exasperation. In his eyes, his sister was dancing with death. She had survived open heart surgery only to come home and pick up a venomous snake. He was sure that she had lost some of her mental faculties. No woman in their right mind would pick up a live Rattlesnake. Before surgery, she feared them and always wore boots. Now, she was standing there barefoot and had been out in the desert that way.

"I am standing still . . . "she squealed back holding the wiggling and curling snake up in the air while she looked about to see what the danger was. With her hands high in the air, she looked like she was being robbed at gunpoint. "What is wrong?"

"You are holding a live Rattlesnake. Its mouth is open . . ." White Eagle stated with both of his hands on the sides of his face in sheer shock and panic. "Don't move till I get a knife to kill it with. When I say so, toss the rattler away from you. I will throw a knife at it. Be calm . . .!" He stated with beads of perspiration running down his face. He was a good shot with a shotgun, but he wasn't sure about his aim with a knife. He was the weak eyed member of the family who wore thick glasses. He suddenly felt the need to pee. She had scared it out of him.

"There is no need to kill it with a knife. I will snap its neck when I am ready to cook it for supper. I will put it in my pillow case in my bedroom till then."

"Holy Mother of God, you have lost it! Don't move Sleeping Moon. Our family has not eaten rattlesnake in over a hundred years. We are ranchers and have a freezer full of steaks, wild boar, and anything else you want to eat. You don't even have to cook. We have a cook. If you want Rattlesnake to eat, I will buy it already dead and frozen."

"What do you mean we have a freezer full of steaks? I always catch a snake for supper and store him in a case or a gunny sack. Do you want me to drop this snake down in a freezer till I am ready to cook him?" she asked a little confused as to her new family's way of doing things.

"Do not move Sis . . . stay calm. I realize you haven't quite been yourself since your surgery. If you want snake for supper, you can have snake for supper. However, I am blowing the hell out of the one you are holding if I can find the housekeeper's pop gun in the drawer next to the spoons." He said suddenly fearing that he couldn't kill the snake with a thrown knife. The rattler was showing his fangs!"

About that time, Night Hawk, their older brother, walked into the kitchen from outside toting a brown cardboard box full of white paper wrapped meats.

"Stop, Night Hawk! Don't get any closer!" White Eagle shouted in a panic holding his hand up to his brother. "Don't get near her or scare her. She is holding a live Rattlesnake."

Night Hawk's mouth dropped open in shock and he gasped. He could see a curling, wiggling Rattlesnake that was shaking its button tail in a rattling frenzy. His sister was holding by the neck one mad rattler.

"Sis . . . I don't know why you are standing in the middle of the kitchen with a live Rattlesnake in your hand. However, don't move. I am going to pull my gun from my boot and take care of it. "He stated slowly sitting down the brown cardboard box of frozen meat on the red tile floor and removing a small revolver from his boot. He then rose slowly not wanting to excite her or the snake. "When I tell you to throw it and run, do it no questions asked! I will shoot the snake when it hits the floor. Do you understand?"

"You are going to blow away my snake?" Sleeping Moon asked excitedly not understanding why they were so bent out of shape.

"They aren't, I am!" stated their eighty-four year old grandmother named Song Bird who walked into the kitchen from the living area. She pulled an antique, two shot pistol from her long, purple, Navajo type full skirt. Faster than the two brothers could gasp, she shot the snake one inch below Moon Dance's hand leaving her holding the Rattlesnake head and about five inches of its body .

Moon Dance, excited from the sound of the gun, threw the head which was still alive toward her first brother over in the kitchen by the knives. He jumped up on to the kitchen counter screaming like a wild Kachina. The Rattlesnake's head with its open mouth flying towards him caused him to wet his jeans. That wasn't a pleasant thing for a twenty- six year old, fearless, Native American Indian man. His grandmother and sister had just scared the pee wad out of him. Even more frightening than the snake was the bullet that went thru the snake and whizzed by his body landing in the wooden front of the kitchen cabinet next to him missing him by half an inch. Any man would pee his pants.

Night Hawk ran to his elderly Indian grandmother and relieved her of the tiny, antique, two shot pistol. He knew she carried it, but she had never had a reason to use it before. He was shocked that she had the strength to pull the trigger. She was also half blind and wore thick glasses like White Eagle. As a rule, she couldn't thread a needle or read a paper without glasses. Half blind best described her.

Grandmother Song Bird had carried the gun in her pocket since she was in her twenties. She was now eighty-four. The boys went along with it thinking it made her feel safe. Putting the tiny hand gun in the pocket of her long Navajo type skirt was a daily habit like putting on your shoes or watch. The tiny gun hadn't been fired probably in fifty years. It had been a gift from her husband when they first bought the ranch. She always feared humming strangers that seemed to roam the nights on their ranch. Her husband had told her it was just border crossers making a run from the border patrol. The hand gun had been purchased to make her feel secure from them.

Night Hawk, seeing that everyone was alright, dropped to his knees with his grandmother's pop gun in his hand. Then he started making the sign of the cross over and over and over shaking his head side to side in unbelief.

"What are you all so damn excited about? I have my glasses on." The elderly Indian woman stated nonchalantly walking over to the kitchen cabinet stepping over the lower half of the dead rattler. She grabbed a banana off the center counter, peeled it, and took a bite. "What are we having for dinner?"

Night Hawk, a raven haired Native American Indian wearing western wear, sat trembling on the red tile floor. The women in his life had almost killed his brother and him before they had a chance to finish sowing their wild oats. They weren't thirty yet. His grandmother could have killed either of them with that antique revolver due to her bad eyesight. He was going to mass first thing in the morning. This brush with death had suddenly made a new man out of him. He might become a priest.

"I was really looking forward to rattlesnake for supper." Sleeping Moon stated looking at her hand that was covered with Rattlesnake blood. I guess I will have to settle for steak. Will you show me where the freezer is so I will know where to store my next snake?"

"Sleeping Moon . . ." Night Hawk stated softly trying not to alarm her. He could tell that her mental faculties apparently had slipped. "You can have anything you want to eat here. We are not poor people. We are ranchers and have credit cards out our backside. You can have anything you want to eat or dine in any restaurant in the valley. You do not need to hunt Rattlesnake or any other wild animal. I will send one of our ranch hands to the supermarket for anything you want, no matter what time of day or night it is. Also, in case you have forgotten, we have a housekeeper and cook named Charlie Elkhorn. You do not need to cook. He is here to serve you and grandmother."

"I am not a provider here?" Moon Dance, now Sleeping Moon, asked not use to being a lady of leisure.

"Your brother, White Eagle, and I are the providers. We run the ranch and make sure our freezers here and in the bunk house are full. Your job is to take care of yourself, spend our money, and be Grandmother Song Bird's companion. You and Grandmother make decisions about redecorating, menus for the cook, and keeping yourself in beauty shop appointments for hair braiding and manicures. We are honorable, wealthy, Native American ranchers and take care of our women. You do not have to work or catch snakes for supper. However, from here on out, your number one responsibility is to make sure I make it to mass on time. God help us, we could have all died today and I haven't been to confession in five years. However, that is changing. I just faced my mortality and I am mending my ways."

"Am I a religious person? I am sure that I believe in a Great Spirit, an Indian one."

"Oh shit," Night Hawk stated shaking his head and turning to White Eagle.

"She doesn't remember her thoughts of becoming a nun."

"Why would I be a nun? If I could choose a religion, I would be a Pentecostal Holy Ghost woman like Three Toes." She stated and then bit her lip. Three Toes was not part of this new human life. He was part of her old existence as Moon Dance in the desert of New Mexico. She was going to have to be more careful and not get her two lives mixed.

"I told you not to let that strange hospital chaplain in to see her. He must have been one of those Pentecostal Holy Roller dancers. She has been converted." White Eagle stated throwing his arms up in exasperation and moving from his frozen position on the kitchen cabinet counter. "She may have just doomed herself to Hell."

"When did you convert?" Grandmother Song Bird asked making the sign of the cross and looking at Sleeping Moon with a confused look on her face. "I sat with you every waking hour that you were in the hospital. I did not see a Holy Ghost Spirit visiting you. "

"I only convert at Christmas, you know, for a charity basket. We always get a canned ham. I will convert back." Sleeping Moon stated once more putting her foot in her mouth. Charity baskets had been a regular welcomed event when she lived with the tribe in the New Mexico desert.

"We do not convert for ham! We have all the wild boar we want! We kill one or two a month. We give to charity, not take it." Night Hawk stated a little pissed. He was not a cheap assed, food stamp taking, reservation Indian who took handouts. He had worked hard to be respected in his community.

"How about chocolate bars. I think I may have converted once upon a time for chocolate bars."

"You don't eat chocolate. You have never eaten chocolate because of your heart condition. You are a lemon drop woman and have been a vegetarian till today."

"Vegetables . . . ? Is that why I am so skinny? Have we been too poor in the past to have meat and chocolate?"

"White Eagle, we will call the doctor first thing in the morning." Night Hawk stated. "Something has gone wrong. She has taken a turn for the crazy side. Maybe her heart doctor can give her something to control the onset of this madness. I will stay with her and sit up with her tonight. I think it best that we not let her out of our sight till we get her in to see the doctor tomorrow. You finish putting the meat away."

"I think I am going to need to change my jeans before I handle our box of meat. I have had a little accident." White Eagle replied turning a little red.

"Oh God, what are you, some sort of piss-pants girl?" Night Hawk asked eyeing the front of his younger brother's jeans.

"Well, you were not the one who had a live Rattlesnake head thrown at you and then a bullet come whizzing and miss you by an inch."

"Come on, Sis. You and I are going to spend the evening watching the big screen and then I am going to grab my Indian flute and woo you to sleep with its sound, just like I did when you were young. I will roll out my sleeping bag and sleep in your room next to your bed. It will be like old times when we were kids."

"May I sleep on the floor too? That bed in my room is a white man's bed. I am not a white man. I am used to sleeping on a rug."

"If you want to sleep on the carpet in your bedroom tonight, that is fine with me. I am sure the doctor will figure out what to do about new medicine for you tomorrow. We will have a sleeping on the carpet night. Right . . . White Eagle?"

"The carpet it is! If she wants a carpet bunking party, I will grab my sleeping bag too . . . after I change my jeans."

CHAPTER SEVEN

HIRING A COMPANION

Night Hawk escorted Sleeping Moon to the doctor the day after the snake incident. The doctor suggested that they find a full time companion for his sister or commit her to a mental institution. Pissed, Night Hawk informed the psychiatrist that he was a quack and that Sleeping Moon would never be placed in a mental institution like a caged wild animal. She just needed some crazy medicine. The decision was made to hire a permanent sitter for Sleeping Moon. The Doctor was agreeable with that and wrote them a couple of prescriptions for a tranquilizer and a sleeper.

So, it was a week after the incident that Night Hawk was speaking on the phone with a neighbor rancher named John Mason.

"How is Jerome doing after his brush with death?" Night Hawk asked.

"I need your help, Night Hawk. Jerome is acting really weird and claiming not to be gay anymore. He wants to go camping, hunt wild boar, and eat barbecue. Does that sound like my Jerome?"

"Perhaps thru his suicide trauma, he has matured and wants to live life differently. Maybe walking up to death's door has caused him to grow up and see what a great father you are." Night Hawk stated pausing to take a sip of coffee from a mug on his desk.

"He is smothering me trying to make up for all the years he ignored me. He claims not to be gay anymore and has purchased a pink gun cabinet for his room. He threw out his sewing machine. He now wants my fishing rod rack to hang over his bed."

"Jerome can't change being gay. Maybe he is just trying to tone it down for your benefit and seeing life from a new perspective."

"He has been hitting my liquor cabinet regularly. I locked it this morning thinking maybe he is diving into a bottle instead of pills now. "

"A shot or two won't hurt him, John. Maybe the drinking on his part is an effort on his part to impress you. I have heard that brushes with death changes you and makes you do strange things. I have started attending mass regularly due to Sleeping Moon and her snake. She and White Eagle could be in their grave tonight. The first time you are over this way, I will show you the bullet that is still imbedded in our kitchen cabinet. It missed White Eagle by half an inch. I have hung a small cross on a nail by the bullet to remind all of us daily how close we came to dying."

"I look at that bed where the paramedics worked on Jerome and I get the willies. I have got to replace the carpet where he threw up enchiladas, beans, and pills on it. I can't get the stain out. It is a sad daily reminder of how close I came to losing him." John Mason replied.

"We are definitely paddling similar canoes, John. I am looking for a live in companion for Sleeping Moon. No one is answering my help wanted add. Song Bird has alienated just about every woman in our area and has ran off droves of house help with her high notes. Charlie Elkhorn has been the only one that has ever stayed past two weeks. He watches out for Song Bird and doesn't take any crap off of her. However, asking him to keep up with two crazy women might send him packing."

"Believe me . . . I understand the hired help problem. I can't find a companion for Jerome either. I am pretty desperate and don't feel I can let him out of my sight for fear of him trying to commit suicide again."

"I don't know what I am going to do John. If Sleeping Moon doesn't kill us with a live snake, Song Bird is going to put a hole thru us with her pea shooter. I have been sleeping in my sleeping bag every night on the floor next to Sleeping Moon's bed in fear of her wandering off into the night snake hunting."

"Desperate times call for desperate measures. I have locked up all of my guns and their bullets I have stored in my money safe of which I had the lock combination changed. I am afraid to leave Jerome alone in fear of him trying it again. None of my ranch hands want to hang out with him because they remember him as an obnoxious gay man who hit on them. I can't take him everywhere I go. A man has to have a little room to breathe and visit the ladies occasionally. Jerome is smothering me trying to be my best friend now. I need help, Night Hawk. Jerome is ruining what little love life I have. I am not young anymore and girlfriends are getting harder to catch."

"Is there anything I can do?"

"Would you consider letting Jerome come stay with you for a week or two while I do my annual branding and selling. I am not turning him loose on my herd or my hired help with a hot branding iron. I just need him safe and out of my hair for a couple of weeks till I get caught up."

"What are you going to use for an excuse to send him to me. He has never been particularly fond of my brother White Eagle. Have you forgot that White Eagle made fun of Jerome's pink pants and pink silk shirt last year at your sister's wedding. I thought your Jerome was going to get the best of White Eagle when he started throwing cups of pink, Vodka spiked punch at him."

"We did have one good time at that wedding, didn't we?" John Mason laughed. "The caterer wasn't too happy. Those crystal cups were his."

"White Eagle still talks about the cup that knocked his western hat off. I don't think he will ever laugh at Jerome's taste in color or clothing anymore. Your Jerome is a little spitfire! "

"What would you say to possibly pretending to hire him for a couple of weeks to keep an eye on your sister? She would be safe with him. We both know that he is gay. It would solve your problem and mine for a short interval while I do what I need to do and you find a permanent sitter for your sister."

"That isn't a bad idea, John. I could ask Grandmother Song Bird to keep an eye on both of them for us. She is old, but still nosey as all hell. Did I tell you that she took that rattler out at sixteen feet with a pea shooter?"

"I wouldn't even attempt that and I won last year's Thanksgiving Turkey Shoot. White Eagle is lucky to still have his yang." John Mason laughed.

"You have got that right."

"Jerome is harmless, Night Hawk. He confessed to trying to kill himself over a male lover who dumped him. I think he and Sleeping Moon might actually enjoy each other's company. However, Jerome might squeal a little and gag if she offers him Rattlesnake stew."

"It sounds like a deal to me. I want you to be sure and tell Jerome to not let her pick up anything deadly and why. He has a yang and Song Bird's next shot at the snake might not be so accurate. A bullet thru Jerome's thing is not my idea of a sex change operation."

"Good point. I will make sure he knows about the Rattlesnake and the pea shooter." John Mason replied laughing.

"Put Jerome on the phone and I will make arrangements with him. I assume you are paying his salary for the two weeks?" Night Hawk asked digging his rich, rancher friend.

"How about we trade adult babysitting services? I will keep Sleeping Moon for two weeks sometime when you want to sow a few wild oats with a lady friend."

"That isn't a bad idea, John. White Eagle and I haven't had a night out since her surgery and all of this craziness started. I have been sleeping in a sleeping bag on my sister's floor. She has definitely lost some of her mental faculties. She is different. It has to be due to the fact they had to perform extreme measures to bring her back when she died on the operating table. Before her surgery, she would have run squealing like a Kachina if she saw a snake."

CHAPTER EIGHT

PINK COW GIRL BOOTS

Moon Dance, who had locked herself in her bedroom for the afternoon, heard a car pulling up the lane approaching the ranch house. She stepped to her bedroom window to see who it was. She had only been on the ranch a couple of weeks and there were so many people that she didn't know. It was difficult to smile and interact with strangers pretending she knew them. She hoped the car wasn't full of prissy ladies from some organization coming to visit her. All the women friends of Sleeping Moon, that she had met so far, were rich, spoiled, and thought the word horse meant a mustang car. Moon Dance, now Sleeping Moon, had gone thru it in the dessert of New Mexico protecting and providing for her all woman tribe of Weelo beings. She had done without food and personal wants to keep her group from being discovered. Sleeping Moon's friends were rich, pampered, naïve, and wasted their money and resources like there was no tomorrow. They didn't have a clue that just one bomb from the Great Mother Ship Noah II could have wiped out all of Canada, the United States, and Mexico. She didn't see idle chatter about manicure appointments and the latest fashion as relevant to reality.

Moon Dance missed her Weelo tribe, even if they had betrayed her. She wondered if the men from the reservation, who had fled to Utah, had managed to make contact with and board the Great Mother Ship. Besides Jack Benson, she wondered if she was the only Weelo left on Planet Earth. She felt so alone and knew that Jack had possibly incarnated in a newborn and it might be years before he made his way to her. She hoped that he had safely incarnated and was well. She did, after some serious thinking, remember him being one of twelve doctors on the Mother Ship thousands of years before, but they hadn't moved about on the ship in the same social circle. He had not been her physician. She vaguely recalled one of her scientist colleagues asking her if she knew she had a stalker. In the back of her mind she remembered turning and looking at a man who was staring at her.

In her new ranch life and Sleeping Moon hell, Moon Dance wasn't sure that she was going to be able to survive. She didn't particularly like the woman that Sleeping Moon had been or her family. White Eagle and Night Hawk were mischief makers and thought outside of the box to see what kind of madness they could pull on each other. The cook, Charlie Elkhorn, was equally as nuts. He had put a life-like, green, plastic frog in the bottom of her oatmeal dish at breakfast to see her jump. She was not fond of frogs. On planet Weelo, they were venomous just like the Rattler on Earth. She took it as a message on his part, that he was out to get her or kill her.

Standing gazing out the window, Moon Dance gave some thought to the possibility that there might be another Weelo out there who had missed their ride home on the rescue craft. She wondered if all the men that had fled to the land of Utah had made it on board. She was considering abandoning her new family that she just did not particularly like. Walking away into the night, she could make her way to Utah in hopes of finding at least one un-rescued Weelo. Perhaps she could pair up with him to survive. She did not see how she could possibly survive with Sleeping Moon's Earth family. She just did not fit in.

It was a very lonely feeling thinking she was possibly alone on Earth and forgotten by the Weelo tribe she once provided for and loved. She felt like a survivor on a desert island with just palm trees and wild animals to keep her company. Humans as a whole were like wild animals. Sleeping Moon's Earth family were wild animals. She secretly hoped and prayed that a male Weelo was out there somewhere. She could start a new tribe with him and possibly give birth to some pure Weelo Children. It was possible since the Earth body of Sleeping Moon was young. She needed a tribe to survive with. She was willing now to mate and give birth to children and a new tribe. Gray Feather was married. She had to move on if she could. She half way regretted not going home on the Great Mother Ship. Her life as Sleeping Moon was distasteful. She hated everything about it.

Moon Dance, now Sleeping Moon, watched as the car pulled up into the driveway on the side of the ranch house next to the kitchen. A wimpy looking little guy about her age got out of the driver's door, retrieved a purple suitcase from the backseat, and then stood eyeing the ranch house. The car he had arrived in sped away back down the lane and out of sight.

"He looks as lost as I feel." Moon Dance muttered. "If he is here for a job as a ranch hand, the men are going to eat him up and spit him out the first two hours. I better go rescue the sissy little dude before the redneck ranch hands discover him." Then she grinned and smirked to herself. "If he is Weelo making his way to me, I am in trouble."

Moon Dance quickly unlocked her bedroom door, started to whistle, and sauntered quickly down the hall and left the ranch house by the kitchen door. She made her way to the side drive where the wimpy, little, pink, prissy stranger stood. He had on pink western boots, blue jeans, pink western shirt, and a purple cowboy hat. The hot pink leather belt in his jeans had pink sequins on it. Moon Dance bit her lip to keep from laughing in front of him.

"May I help you?" she asked eyeing him.

"My name is Harley. Are you Song Bird? I am here to apply for the position as a companion to some sick cactus flower named Sleeping Moon."

"I am Sleeping Moon." Moon Dance answered totally amused. The pink booted dude probably couldn't take care of himself, much less someone that was seriously ill. "Why do you wish to be my companion?" She asked looking him directly in the eye and suddenly seeing Weelo eyes staring back at her.

Harley slid his pink, poke-a-dot sunglasses down to the end of his nose and stared into her eyes. "Moon Dance, is that you?"

Moon Dance began to belly laugh. "I gather you found a body to travel in. Isn't your taste in human vehicles a little extreme?"

"Don't laugh! You are walking around in one that is bowlegged. What is that all about? Have you been riding too many horses or who knows what?" Jack Benson shot back annoyed. He then started fanning himself with a pink handkerchief that he removed from his shirt pocket.

"I am bow legged?"She asked in shock. Looking down, she pulled up her mid-calf length skirt to look. She was bow legged.

"I could shoot a basketball thru them and never touch your skin. Your new body is definitely a step down from that of Moon Dance. She was a ten in her seventies. You are twentyish and possibly a four or a five maybe. You definitely need to wear skirts to hide those legs."

Insulted and with tears springing up in her s eyes, she replied in a huff. "Well, you are no prize either, you wimpy little piece of cross dresser crap. On a scale of one to ten on the male scale, you are possible a minus five or below. You don't even rate in my book. You look like a cheap ass, gay, little tramp of a Saturday night cow girl."

"Ouch! I look that bad?" he asked also starting to tear up looking down at himself. "I wanted to dress like a male coming here, but this outfit was all there was in the wrecked car's suitcase. A girl has to do what a girl has to do. I haven't had a chance to get to town yet and buy myself some male clothes."

"Well, join the club. I haven't had a chance to have my legs straightened. Why did you pick that body, Jack Benson? Are you nuts?"

"My twenty four hours were about up. I couldn't find a new conception or a dying adult to take over. I was floating down the main drag in Las Vegas heading for the hospital to look around when I spotted a serious car wreck. A cross dresser dude had wrecked his convertible and was kissing a light pole. It was a take it or leave it situation. I only had an hour left and I was not taking any chances. I had to find my way back to you."

"Come on in and let me introduce you to Charlie Elkhorn our housekeeper and cook. I will tell him that you are my choice for a companion and that I have hired you. You realize you and I are going to be living with redneck Native Americans who live and breathe to prank each other. I am going to have to protect you or you won't last ten minutes here. I knew better than to leave you on your own to find a body. Only a mother or I could care about you in that getup." She said shaking her head and walking around him, taking the grand tour.

Jack Benson reached out and took her hand in his nicely manicured male one and squeezed it with expression saying, "I am a doctor, a psychiatrist, remember? I can hold my own with your new family."

"I thought I was a survivor and tough. These yahoos have me locking my bedroom door and in tears."

"No tears, Moon Dance. I am here." He said squeezing her hand. "I also have some news for you. I ran across a light port up towards Vegas. Should we ever want to return to Weelo; we can take it. It looks like a round glass elevator. I watched two purple skinned spirits enter it."

"Where?" She asked letting go of his hand.

"At first I thought it was one of those huge spotlights they flash in the sky displaying casino bill boards. When I got up close to it floating over this area heading towards Vegas, I realized it was a light beam port and exits on top of a barn like structure. I wasn't paying too close of attention as to its location. I was in a hurry. I just know it is near here." He replied and then added taking another look at her legs. "It is a good thing I am a basketball hoop man. Only I could appreciate those legs."

"Well wimp, it looks like you and my bow legs are in this mess together. Now concerning the light port, I am aware plutonian beings use light ports to arrive and exit on Planet Earth. They were experimenting with them thousands of years ago when the Great Mother Ship, Noah I crashed. From what I remember of the studies and experiments back then, the purple pigment in plutonian skin activates their ports. You or I would not be able to travel in their port without one of them accompanying us. Plus, only two at a time can use the ports. Do you know a Plutonian?"

"I see." He stated."Your flight engineer degree is kicking in. Do you know a Plutonian on Earth or the other side who would be willing to come by light port for us?"

"No, I am sorry that I don't. The only Plutonian here that I have been privileged to meet was the one using Sleeping Moon's body. I talked with her shortly before she took her light port home. She turned this body over to me to use. Plutonian do usually travel in pairs. It is possible that her traveling companion is still here occupying a human body vehicle somewhere in the area. However, she didn't mention anyone." Moon Dance stated. "You and I will have to wait for a Weelo rescue ship and that might take many lifetimes and many incarnations."

"Well, take me inside and let us get this incarnation show on the road. I will show you that I can hold my own with your yahoos."

"Well, Benson, you are about to meet a prejudiced family of red necks. The cook is going to hate you just as much as he hates me. By the way, pink is definitely not your color." She stated giggling looking him over.

"Gee . . . thanks! It is not like I had a chance to consult a color expert before coming here. When you incarnate you get what you get. This is what the cross dresser had on when he crashed his convertible and kissed the light pole."

Moon Dance pointed to the back door and headed that way. Harley Jack Benson followed her into the ranch house after picking up his purple suitcase. Just as they were stepping into the center of the kitchen, Charlie Elkhorn, the cook, stepped in from the pantry where the freezer was. Seeing a stranger in his kitchen, he instantly drew a magnum from the waist of his belt.

"State your business here, pink boy. Step to one side Sleeping Moon. I will shoot the sucker if he makes a move on you."

"Oh, sweetie . . . I am not going to make a move on her. However, if you are available I would be interested. I like a man in an apron. You should let me design you one that fits your body better and pick a color that is right for your eyes. I can just see you now in a mustard yellow one with pink butterflies all over it. You would be one hot – hot – hunk. Delicious might be a better word." Harley Jack Benson stated licking his lips.

"What . . . ?" Charlie Elkhorn gasped with a shocked look on his face. He had just been hit on by a she-he stranger. "I am going to dunk you in a pile of mustard yellow hog slop, you little prick. Where have you come from and why are you in my kitchen?"

Moon Dance was at a loss for words as Benson pulled off his she-he act annoying the hell out of the cook. In a way, she was half way delighted. Charlie Elkhorn had put a fake green frog in the bottom of her oatmeal bowl at breakfast. She didn't appreciate it since she hated frogs. Rattlesnakes she liked. She would have thought it quite amusing if he had put a tiny plastic snake in her bowl of oatmeal slop.

"Oh sweet thing, I am Sleeping Moon's new companion. We are going to be having bunking parties, late night hair coloring sessions, and hopefully chocolate

Bonbons to snack on. Hopefully, you are an accomplished enough chef to make them. You look like a backstreet diner cook to me. If you are just a cook, I will teach you how to make Bonbons! I personally am a high class, fine dining chef and could possibly show you a thing or two after dinner, if you know what I mean. It takes a hot pink girl to make a real Bonbon out of a man. You look like a vanilla Bonbon to me. However, I can see you as a strawberry pink coated Bonbon that I would like to take a nibble of or dip in chocolate. You are one sweet looking thing."

Charlie Elkhorn flew to the cabinet and grabbed a meat tenderizing hammer from the utensil rack and raised it. Sleeping Moon quickly stepped in front of wimpy, little Harley Jack Benson to protect him from six foot two, hundred and eighty pound, Native American Charlie Elkhorn who was fuming mad.

"Get out of my way, Sleeping Moon. That little piece of pink, he-she crap has made homey insinuations toward me. I am going to flatten his Bonbon insinuating lips and then pound him up into steak and fry him."

"Is that a promise, Sweetie? Right after supper would be better timing. I could nibble my Bonbon lips all over your yummy face." Harley Jack Benson stated crouched and hiding behind Moon Dance peeping around.

Forgetting Moon Dance, Charlie Elkhorn made a dash for Harley Jack Benson and was chasing him in circles around Moon Dance when Grandmother Song Bird entered the kitchen. She pulled her antique two shot pop gun from her pocket, aimed it above Charlie's head, and pulled the trigger.

Totally surprised, Charlie and Moon Dance instantly dropped prostrate onto the floor remembering how bad her sight was. Moon Dance wondered how Song Bird had managed to get her gun and bullets back from Night Hawk. Round two of old west gunfire was happening.

"Not today, Charlie Elkhorn, if you want to keep your job here. Fancy Pants there is Sleeping Moon's new companion. Didn't you hear him tell you so? I whistled in my bedroom and the dream catcher above my bed caught him and drew him here. We need a safe companion to sleep in Sleeping Moon's bedroom. He is a girl."

"That pink piece of crap you call Fancy Pants just hit on me. What am I going to do, carry a bull whip and keep my bedroom door locked at night? Sleeping Moon may be safe, but what about me?" Charlie Elkhorn asked in a mad huff.

"Get over it Elkhorn. When Fancy Pants sees Night Hawk and White Eagle, he will forget all about you. They are the chic magnets around here. Fancy Pants will fall for one of them and ignore you. They have got looks and money."

Charlie Elkhorn grinned and sat up in the middle of the floor and crossed his legs. "You are right, Song Bird! White Eagle and Night Hawk are definitely his type. There will be Bonbons for dinner tonight and Fancy Pants will be seated next to Night Hawk. At breakfast in the morning, I will seat him next to White Eagle. May I ask the foreman to eat breakfast with us in the morning too? It will be a morning this ranch will never forget, one that I can tell about at the upcoming powwow. We have been short of good stories lately. "

"I am glad you are seeing the brilliance in Sleeping Moon's choice of Fancy Pants." Grandmother Song Bird stated grinning."I seem to remember my grandsons giving my male lover a ride home in a horse trailer last year in his birthday suit. It is payback time. Fancy Pants is my way of doing so."

"Peace, Song Bird. Put down your weapon and we will smoke the peace pipe. I have a cigar up in the cabinet that I have been reserving for a special moment. I think this must be it." He stated rising from his seated position and leaving the meat hammer on the floor. He walked over to the cabinet and opened the top cabinet door above the dishwasher and pulled down a long, brown, chunky cigar and removed its cellophane wrapper. Then he bit the end off, lit it, took a drag or so on it to get it started and then held it out to the elderly grandmother. Song Bird took a couple of drags off of it and handed it back. She exhaled the thick smelly cigar smoke.

"Peace, Charlie Elkhorn. May I ask why you thought Fancy Pants was a danger to Sleeping Moon?"

"I thought he was an illegal, Mexican border crosser who had possibly broken in on Moon Dance. We do live on the bank of the Rio Grande in case you have forgotten. That is why we all carry a handgun."

"You thought Fancy Pants here was a border crosser? Are you nuts, Elkhorn? He couldn't sneak across the road in that pink madness he is wearing, much less cross the Rio Grande. "

Charlie Elkhorn went to laughing. "You are right Grandmother Song Bird. He is not danger . . . or won't be once he lays eyes on Night Hawk. Fancy-pants is welcome in my kitchen. Besides, if I were a homey, I definitely wouldn't choose a wimpy little piece of pink crap like him. I would get me one of those tall, Las Vegas floor show dancers who wear feathers and spikes. Fancy Pants here just doesn't have it going on."

Harley Jack Benson broke out into a wail and some fake sobbing which Moon Dance was totally amused at. This was a side of Benson that she hadn't anticipated. He was a pretty good actor.

"You are all insensitive Native American Kachina who are trying to make me feel bad about who I am and kill my little pink spirit. I will never forgive you for this Elkhorn. I just don't know what I saw in you when I entered this kitchen.

My love affair with you has been a short one. You are probably impotent anyway. Most six foot jerks are. "

Then Charlie Elkhorn lost it. Forgetting Grandmother Song Bird and her hand-gun, he flew towards Benson in a rage. The peace treaty was a short one. He balled up his fist to knock Harley Jack Benson out.

"I am going to show you who is the man in this kitchen, you little pink booted prick."

Then a second gunshot sounded and a bullet struck the red tiled floor at Charlie's feet scaring the crap out of him. He froze. Harley Jack Benson hid once more behind Moon Dance who had risen from the floor.

"I am sorry Song Bird . . . I have broken our treaty. Let us puff the peace cigar again while Sleeping Moon removes Fancy Pants from my kitchen. Put your pea shooter back in your skirt pocket and let us all live to raid another sunrise."

Grandmother Song Bird put her little gun back in her pocket and then looked at Charlie Elkhorn who was standing frozen and big eyed. Charlie Elkhorn was shaking and horrified. He had almost gone to meet the Great Spirit in the sky with an unwanted sex change operation. That bullet had bounced off the floor and then traveled between his legs way too close to his manhood for comfort.

"Damn it Charlie Elkhorn. Don't kill Fancy Pants before we get the chance to introduce him to White Eagle and Night Hawk. Do you want to spoil a good story for the next campfire? Wouldn't you love to tell about how White Eagle and Night Hawk met and were chased by a She-He Kachina? No prank as good as this has come along for years. You will go down in history when our tribe's story teller hears your tale."

Charlie turned and walked back to the cabinet and picked up the smoking cigar that he had left on the edge of the sink. He then once more handed it to Song Bird. "You are right. I will suck it up till we pull this one off, just keep him out of my kitchen is all I ask. Do so and I will make you a batch of chocolate chip cookies and leave them in your bedroom. You know that you are not to have them. It will be our secret."

"You have a deal, Charlie Elkhorn." Song Bird returned and then turned to Harley. "By the way, Fancy Pants, what is your name?"

"My name is Harley Jack Benson. My lover in Las Vegas, Jerome Mason, gave me your name. Has he shown you the hot photo of us on the back of his steaming pink motorcycle? I know that all of you rich ranchers are friends. I am sad to have to admit that I am desolate and Jerome and I are now history. He went crazy and tried to kill himself. I hope I am not being indiscrete or vulgar, but I just cannot deal with crazy. Jerome has money, but I got none of it before he pulled the trigger. He left me high and dry and now I am a working girl. I am also shopping for a sugar daddy; possibly a sweet smelling cigar man like Charlie Elkhorn. I do love the smell of a good cigar on a man."

"Come on Harley, now!" stated Moon Dance grabbing him by the hand and forcefully pulling him down the hall leading to her bedroom where she pushed him inside her door and quickly locked it for his safety.

"Was I good?" Jack Benson, now Harley, asked leaning on the door and laughing.

"Charlie Elkhorn is going to rip you a new . . . if you keep flaunting yourself and teasing him." Moon Dance laughed leaning against her door with him. "You had me believing you were interested in him."

"I was good, wasn't I?" Harley Jack Benson asked removing his purple western hat and tossing it on her bed. "I was a cast member of the University's drama productions when I was young. I think I pulled the She-He act off pretty good, if I do say so myself."

"You can turn the acting on and off, but that body you have chosen is permanent. You have got to live with it." Moon Dance snickered. "You are at least a head shorter than me."

"Well, bow legs; look at yourself before pointing a finger at my flaws. Inside this body is one heck of a man who could really love you if you would let me?" Jack Benson replied plopping down on her bed and kicking off his pink boots. "Do I get the left or the right side?"

"Neither! You get the floor and a sleeping bag and please quit using the word love. It is not part of my vocabulary anymore."

"How about I substitute the word adore. I do adore the Moon Dance that lives in that bowlegged body you have chosen. "

Moon Dance looked at him and grinned. "Adore is a good word, Harley Jack Benson? However, my ability to feel for a man is shattered as well as my heart. I have trust issues."

"We will work the issues out. I am or was a Psychiatrist, remember?"

"I was once a research scientist and flight engineer, but that doesn't mean much in our current situation." Moon Dance shot back.

"You need my adoring eyes and arms. I will look over your dig at you being more brilliant and intelligent than me. It isn't your mind I am interested in, anyway. I think I just might be attracted to those bow legs of yours." He stated lying down on her pillow and grinning.

"You are awful, Harley Jack Benson. However, adore is a good word and it sounds nice coming from your mouth. I will have to admit, I adore the actor in you. "

"That is a start!" he replied patting the bed next to him. "Come tell me all about your life here so I will know what to expect when we unlock the bedroom door."

Moon Dance crawled upon the bed next to him and laid her head down on his arm. She needed him. He wrapped his arms around her and held her as she told him about her crazy new life.

For the next week, Moon Dance and Harley Jack Benson got to know each other and became inseparable. To annoy White Eagle, Night Hawk, and Charlie Elkhorn; Jack constantly did his he/she act hitting on whichever one of the men was in his presence driving them crazy. After a day or so, the men cleared the room when Harley entered. They left him alone with Moon Dance feeling she was safe with him. Harley Jack Benson slept in Moon Dance's room and in her bed. She clung to him in the night crying. She needed a time to grieve and a shoulder to cry on. He gave to her what she needed. He just held her. His time would come to make love to her when her grief over Gray Feather was over. He was a psychiatrist. He knew that one day she would move on and he would be there to love her.

By the end of the week, Harley Jack and Moon Dance Sleeping Moon started hanging out in the family room watching movies. She seemed to be crying less and enjoying their time together. Harley Jack Benson was pleased that they were bonding. He wanted that because he was in love with her. Then an unexpected, disaster of a visitor showed up at the ranch house throwing a kink In Harley Jack Benson's love life.

CHAPTER NINE

JERI ANN JEROME ARRIVES

A knock sounded at the back door of the ranch house kitchen. Charlie Elkhorn, the cook, left the steaks he was preparing for dinner to answer it. When he opened the door, he was shocked to see another version of Harley standing there. He took a deep breath and prepared himself for another bad encounter with a cross dressing, he/she fruitcake.

"What do you want?" Charlie asked roughly not giving the new male in purple women's wear a chance to start in on him.

Taken back, Jeri Ann Jerome Mason slid his purple poke-a-dot sunglasses down to the end of his nose and took a serious look at the rude cook. "I am here to stay for two weeks as a house guest and companion for Sleeping Moon. Night Hawk invited me."

"We have already hired someone as a companion for Sleeping Moon and don't give me the Night Hawk song and dance. He doesn't hang out with pieces of wimpy, purple she/he crap like you. Don't waste my time. I am in the middle of cooking dinner. Harley, Sleeping Moon's new companion, is enough madness for this house. Now, go away." Elkhorn stated roughly.

"Harley? You have a pink, fancy pants Harley living here?"

"Yes, so be on your way. Our position is filled."

"The companion position is mine. I am Jeri Ann Jerome Mason, John Mason's son. Night Hawk sent for me. Don't mess with me or I will tell my father and he will call in the note Night Hawk owes him and you will be without a job." He replied eyeing the rude cook.

"You are John Mason's son Jerome?" Charlie Elkhorn asked a little confused. He couldn't imagine Night Hawk inviting another pink pants man to drive them all crazy.

Night Hawk had quit eating in the ranch house due to Harley continuously hitting on him. He took his dinner down in the bunkhouse with the ranch hands every night. He privately told Elkhorn that Harley was history as soon as he could find someone else to hire to watch Sleeping Moon.

"Oh . . . you are a replacement for Harley. Come on in, Jerome."

"I am glad I got my point across. Now retrieve my luggage for me and show me where I am to sleep. I expect my breakfast at ten and served to me in my bedroom on your best china. I am not a plastic plate person. Scoot to it getting my bags from the drive where our ranch foreman unloaded them. I don't want some low class ranch dog of yours using them for a fire hydrant. You will carry them in, open them, and put my clothes away in the guest room. Then you will make me a cup of hot tea with a wedge of lemon on the side and exactly three drops of honey in it. Tea bags are not acceptable. I drink only brewed tea in a tea pot with a cozy to warm it. Please heat my tea cup. I hate a cold tea cup."

Oh shit!" Elkhorn stated shaking his head.

"I do not appreciate words of vulgarity used in my presence; neither would my rich Jewish doctor fiancé. Please refrain from your low class vocabulary. You are looking at a woman of class, not back street, vulgar speaking, street trash."

"Come on in, Miss or Mr. Mason whichever you prefer. I will call down to the bunkhouse and tell Night Hawk you are here. Sleeping Moon and Harley are down the hall in the family room. At least you don't hit on me. That is an improvement over Harley. I am sure that Night Hawk will fire Harley as soon as he knows you are here. Make yourself at home." He stated and then muttered to himself." What have I done to deserve my current Jerome and Harley Hell? I will go to mass and confession tomorrow. Maybe a few 'Hail Mary's' will make them go away."

"Thank you, Mr. Elkhorn. May I ask which end of the Elk you were named after?" Jerome asked eyeing tall masculine Indian cook who had a cigar hanging from his mouth.

"Neither . . ." Charlie Elkhorn growled. "I killed Santa's reindeer before turning the age of one by throwing my baby bottle at him. By the age of two, I shot an Elk's horns off with a bean flipper. By the age of three, I was butchering and grilling little assholes like you. Does that answer your question? You are about to lose your cross dressing antlers if you get my drift."

"Perhaps I might like a man who can keep reindeer in line. What are you doing later tonight, after the cooking is done? A little fling never hurt a girl. We just won't tell my fiancé, Charlie Elkhorn. May we sing 'Here Comes Santa Claus' when we are making love? Should I leave a fifty dollar tip on your pillow or are you a two hundred dollar man?"

"Oh God help me . . ." Charlie Elkhorn muttered trying to control his fist. "Get out of my sight you little piece of rich, Mason Ranch crap. My kitchen is off limits to you. If you don't like it, take it up with Night Hawk. He is down in the bunkhouse. I am sure that he and the ranch hands can answer any questions you have or solve any problems you have got. I am the ranch cook and this is my kitchen. You would have to pay five thousand for me."

"Oh . . . You must be one hell of a man, Charlie Elkhorn. I will ask my father for my spending allowance. We are on!"

Charlie Elkhorn was just about at the point of losing it. However, the Masons were the richest family in the valley and you didn't mess with them. He didn't want to lose his job, because he was in love with Sleeping Moon. He was going to have to suck it up and stay clear of Jerome.

"Don't speak to me unless you have five thousand in cash to lay down on my kitchen cabinet. Furthermore, we drink coffee here. If you want a heated cup of lemon tea, call your ranch and have your cook send it over along with your maid to serve it. A cup of black Joe is all you are getting from me and you will have to pour it yourself. The coffee maker is on the end of the cabinet. I have two duties here and that is to cook and look after Song Bird. You will have to provide your own maid service."

"I like a man who tells me what is what. Do you keep a whip in your bedroom? Is that why your services are worth so much? "Jeri Ann Jerome whined in a sticky flirty voice.

"Harley and Sleeping Moon are back in the family room. Go back there and join them before I lose my temper and take my meat cleaver to you."

"Aren't you attracted to me?" Jeri Ann Jerome asked not flinching.

"You just are not my type Miss or Mr. Mason. I go for girls in pink. The purple you have on just doesn't do it for me. I prefer Harley who is in the back with Sleeping Moon. Go check him/her out."

"The Harley man back in the family room, should I take the time to freshen up before I meet him? Is he a motorcycle rider? Is that why you call him Harley?"

"You are just as fresh as he is, believe me. Leave your purse on the hook by the kitchen door. That is where everyone leaves their coats and things when entering the ranch house this direction. Starting tomorrow, you will remove your shoes when you enter my kitchen and leave them outside the door on the mud porch. I am not into mopping up filth after wimps like you. You will carry your own weight around here or provide a maid to do so."

"I will help you mop if you want, for free. You put one hand on the handle,

Charlie Elkhorn, and I will put one. We could be good at handle holding."

"Get out of here before I throw you out." Charlie Elkhorn stated balling up his right fist. "You make one more insinuation to me and I am going to personally send you home to the Mason ranch as hamburger meat."

"Tut-tut . . . you have a temper, Mr. Elkhorn. I must pray for you ever night before I go to bed."

"Who do you pray to, the Devil?" Charlie muttered while thinking that he had just embarked on a new two week journey into hell. He wasn't sure he wasn't going to survive the onslaught of pink fancy pant demons that had showed up on the doorstep of his kitchen.

Jeri Ann Jerome Mason removed his shoes and placed them by the back door and hung his huge purple handbag on a coat hook on the rack that was attached to the wall next to the door. Then he headed down the hall toward the family room. Just before entering the family room, he recognized a familiar voice. It sounded like his ex-lover Harley from Las Vegas, yet it also sounded like jack Benson. That was not possible. He peeped into the family room and saw Harley, his ex-lover sitting with Moon Dance on a love seat sharing a big bowl of popcorn while watching a movie.

"You witch!" screamed Jeri Ann Jerome suddenly charging into the room. How dare you make your way here and weasel in on my friends looking for a handout. You stole my address book containing my rich friends' addresses. This is low of you Harley, conning my wealthy friends. What happened to Poodle Boy? Did he dump you for the garbage truck driver?"

Jack Benson, now in Harley's body, jumped to his feet recognizing Jeri Ann Jerome's voice. He didn't reply because he didn't want her recognizing his voice and possibly spoiling his new relationship with Moon Dance. He knew sure as hell, Jeri Ann Jerome would tell Moon Dance about him kissing her when they were in spirit form. His kiss was a spur of the moment thing and didn't mean anything. He was now in an unexpected situation he didn't know how to get out of.

"I see the cat has got your tongue?" Jeri Ann Jerome smirked. "Don't you have anything to say for yourself? You stole my mustang, pink boots, and broke my heart dumping me for Poodle Boy. Now you are trying to screw my friends." Jerome Jeri Ann shouted with his/her face turning red. Next to Jeri Ann Jerome was a table with a stack of magazines on it. Spotting them, she started to screech and throw magazines at Harley across the room.

Moon Dance jumped up and ran for cover behind an oversized chair. The magazines were flying like predator, mad hawks and she wondered what was next and who the hell was the mad man dressed in purple women's wear was.

Jack Benson did not answer Jeri Ann Jerome. He ran for the back of a chair also.

"What do you want and who are you?" yelled Moon Dance. She didn't have a clue as to who Jeri Ann Jerome was. She had only been living in Sleeping Moon's body for a couple of months.

"I am Jeri Ann Jerome Mason. Your brothers want some time to spend with their ladies away from here. They have hired me for two weeks to baby sit you. You are crazy in case you don't know it and so is Song Bird. I have been hired to be your baby sitter and you better not give me any grief. Charlie Elkhorn is Song Bird's permanent sitter."

"My brothers want you to baby sit me?" Moon Dance asked aghast.

"The two of you have a reputation for being off the wall crazy. Since your surgery, Night hawk says you have the onset of some serious mental problems due to oxygen loss during your heart surgery. You did die you know. You can't help it that you came back without some of your mental faculties."

Jack Benson still wasn't saying a word. He started crawling around the furniture trying to make his way toward a set of French doors he planned to open and then quickly exit. He couldn't let Jeri Ann discover who he was or let Moon Dance find out he had kissed her.

"Where are you going?" Jeri Ann Jerome asked turning his attention to Harley Jack Benson. "Are you afraid to have to explain yourself in front of Sleeping Moon?

Still Jack Benson didn't answer. Caught heading in a crawl toward the French doors, he scooted backwards behind the chair once more.

"Just tell us what you want and then quit throwing stuff." Moon dance yelled as another hawk like magazine flew across the room. "Harley and I are friends. Song Bird hired him to be my companion. I do not need a babysitter. You can go back and tell my brothers and your father that."

"Well, I can see that I am not wanted here. I will just go home and tell my father that you have treated me really badly. I am sure he won't make that three hundred thousand dollar loan to your brothers for cattle after he hears how you have treated me."

"Wait . . . !" Moon Dance shouted. "We are not trying to do anything to rock the boat between your dad and my brothers. I can have two friends . . . er . . . uh . . . . baby sitters."

"I am out of here as soon as I extract blood and everything from Harley that belongs to me. Stand up and face me like a man, you Poodle Boy lover." Jeri Ann Jerome yelled throwing two more magazines and then picking up a lamp.

"I am not a man!" Jack Benson in Harley's body yelled losing his cool. "I am a girl, remember?"

"In my thinking, you are a witchy little coward and thief." Jeri Ann Jerome yelled throwing the lamp. It crashed violently against the stone fireplace making a terrible noise and then shattered into multiple pieces.

"Benson," whispered Moon Dance crawling and taking refuge behind the same chair he was behind. "When I say go, run for the French doors. I will be right behind you protecting your backside. My bedroom window is open. Run around the house, climb thru it, and hide. I am going to throw things at her till you have a chance to escape. Be ready to help me in the window when I make a run for it. I am sure she is going to be one mad, pissed off, female Rattlesnake."

"I am ready," he said as a crystal vase whizzed by above the chair they were behind. It crashed against a wall. Flowers and water flew everywhere.

Moon Dance spotted a basket of yarn balls belonging to Song Bird next to the chair she was behind. She suddenly had a weapon at her disposal. She took a deep breath and grabbed the basket of yarn balls.

Jumping to her feet, Moon Dance shouted to Jack Benson, "Go!" She then bombarded Jeri Ann Jerome with yarn balls one after the other. Jeri Ann Jerome squealed seeing all the colored objects coming toward him and ran down the hall toward the kitchen yelling, "Elkhorn, save me! . . . Save me! Sleeping Moon has gone crazy!"

Moon Dance shot out the French doors right after Benson. She hurried around the house and practically dove into her bedroom window like it was a swimming hole and then pulled down the sash and closed the drapes. Then she sat down on her carpeted bedroom floor beneath the window snickering.

"I have not had that much fun since I was a kid. "Benson stated sitting down beside her and joining her in quiet, snorting laughter. "I adore you, Moon Dance."

"I think I adore you too, Benson." She replied taking his hand in hers and squeezing it. "Just so you know, I can read your mind. Weelo women have that ability. You don't have to worry about kissing Jerri Ann Jerome. We all do stupid spur of the moment things at times."

"Oh crap, you know about that?"

"I can read your mind. You are like an open book to me."

"You can read my mind . . ."

"Yes, I am afraid you are at my mercy. I can also hear you telling me that you love me."

Jack Benson grinned. "I adore you with my eyes and love you with my heart."

"I can live with you having kissed Jeri Ann if you can live with me for being a fool over Gray feather."

Jack Benson took Moon Dance in his arms and held her to him nuzzling his face to hers. "I want to kiss you, Moon dance. However, I would prefer to do it in a body that is worthy of kissing you. How do you feel about my choosing a new vehicle to travel in?"

"I was thinking the same thing, Benson. I would like to kiss you, but in a body that I feel is worthy. Did you know that Sleeping Moon was a lesbian?"

"We are a pair aren't we?" Benson laughed holding her tight.

"How about we just lie down on the bed and hold each other till Jeri Ann Jerome leaves. Then if you are willing, we will walk away from this ranch and its madness. When we reach a large city we will unzip, discard these bodies, and choose more appropriate ones. I am not crazy about Sleeping Moon's body or her human family." Moon Dance stated. "Should I decide to make love to you, I want it to be with a woman's body that desires a man."

"I would prefer to make love to you with a male body that prefers a woman," he replied holding her tightly and kissing her on her cheek. "I adore you and I will wait to love you till the time is right. I want our adoring of each other to be right."

"If I had waited for you to arrive in my life, I would not have a Gray Feather nightmare to deal with. I would have memories of only you. I am sorry, Benson."

"Whatever our problems are, Moon Dance, we will work thru them. I adore you."

CHAPTER TEN

THE DREAM CATCHER ADVENTURE

Moon Dance and Jack Benson dozed off wrapped in each other's arms. Somewhere between waking and sleeping, a portal to the in-between worlds opened. Jack Benson rose from the sleeping body known as Harley and then helped Moon Dance rise from hers. Hand in hand, floating in mid air like angels at ceiling level, they looked down at their sleeping human bodies.

Jack, in filmy blue spirit form, squeezed the blue sheer hand of Moon Dance's spirit. He was in love with her and had been for centuries. Moon Dance without her bow legged human body was absolutely gorgeous. She had beautiful medium blue skin and three eyes instead of two. One was in the middle of her forehead and it was just as beautiful as her two normal ones.

"You are the most beautiful creature I have ever laid eyes on. My eyes adore you!" Jack Benson said eyeing her. Taking her blue hand with crystal fingernails, he raised it to his lips and kissed it gently and with passion. Moon Dance's filmy blue chiffon type gown floated about her with grace. Her bare blue feet with crystal toenails protruded from the bottom of her gown. Her ears were crystal and she had waist long black hair that was loose and blowing in a supernatural breeze from somewhere.

Moon Dance squeezed Jack Benson's hand back. "You aren't so bad yourself. I like that you are taller than me. It makes me feel safe. I want so much to fall in love with you Benson. You are everything a Weelo woman should want in a man. I am sorry that I was so foolish and gave my heart to a human. I can see in your eyes that you mean it when you say 'I adore you.' It is I who should say that and more. You have no baggage. I come with much. You deserve a Weelo woman with a heart that is whole to love you. "

"I have made my way to you Moon Dance. The great flood separated us before we had a chance to discover each other and mate back then. Now, we have been given another chance. I do not hold Gray Feather against you. All of us ship wrecked Weelo had to mate and do what we needed to do to survive down thru the centuries. If it hadn't been for Gray Feather coming to my office and discussing his memories of you, I wouldn't have made my way here to the desert and you. He is part of a greater plan. Think of him that way. "

"Give me time, Benson. I just don't know how to deal with my foolish act of loving Gray Feather. I am a Weelo Scientist as well as a flight engineer and doctor. I have not acted intelligently in the heart department. I was an old fool in the New Mexico desert and Gray Feather was my folly."

"Come, our human bodies sleep. Let us travel thru the dream catcher's web and see where it takes us."

"Do you think we can get thru it without the hands of the web snaring us? It is a forbidden door."

"Let us give it a try. The most the hands of the web can do is catch us and throw us back into our human bodies."

"That is true. How do we shrink ourselves to the size of the web openings? The dream catcher isn't any bigger than a fruit jar lid."

"Whistling or humming a note from high to low! You are good at whistling. Start at the highest note you can reach and then lower the note to the lowest you can go. As the note lowers, our spirit Weelo bodies will shrink till we are the size of flies and we can travel thru the web of the dream catcher."

"Is that why I have whistled all of these years?" She asked looking at the very small dream catcher with a loose woven web on it.

"You have been traveling thru a nightmare of human existence. Whistling has shrunk your spirit within you and let you hide from the many hands that have wanted to betray you. On the count of three, start to whistle a high note and I will join you. When you reach your low note, fly thru the dream catcher and wait for me on the other side. My low note will be lower, so it will take me a moment or so longer to fly thru. However, I will be right behind you. One . . . two . . . three . . ." He started counting.

Moon Dance hit the highest note she could and then started lowering it. As she did, her spirit form started shrinking till it was the size of a fly. She proceeded to fly towards the catcher. She could see thousands of little minute hands reaching and grabbing trying to ensnarl her as she shot thru one of the web openings. She then turned to see Jack Benson shooting thru a web opening with all of the hands trying to grab him. He made it thru safely. She grabbed his hand and squeezed it in relief and then let it go.

Looking around, Moon Dance realized she was in the sky over the Seven Moons

Jo Hammers

Ranch house looking down. She also saw that there seemed to be a clear force field between her and it. The force field looked like a sheet of running water. It was evident they would have to travel back thru the scary dream catcher with all of its grabbing hands to get back home to her bedroom. "What now, Jack Benson?"

About that time, their conversation was interrupted by a pink human spirit form shooting into their presence angry and shouting at them. "Why did you take my body? It is not yours to have." The spirit sputtered getting in their face.

"Who are you talking about?" Moon Dance retorted asking in shock. "I have permission to travel in Sleeping Moon's body."

"Not you, him!" The female human spirit stated flying circles around them. "Now, I can't re-enter it unless he gives it back to me or if the hands of the web lets me enter and keeps him out."

"Your human body was abandoned and kissing a light pole when I found it." Benson stated in a loud firm voice to the human spirit who was having a hissing fit.

"That may be, but it is still mine. I was thrown violently out of it and landed two blocks away. When I figured out where my body was and made my way back to it, I found you in it. You are a thief!"

"I am not a thief. You were not there when I found and claimed your abandoned human vehicle."

"Well, I want it back!" The human spirit demanded folding its filmy flesh colored arms across its chest. "I am Harley, not you." Then the spirit being of Harley went to wailing and crying a river of tears which ran down into the force field that looked like a sheet of running water.

"I am sorry, Harley. However, I am not giving your body back to you. I need it to watch out for Moon Dance till we go home to Planet Weelo. You can have it back then, if you want. For now, I am saying to you 'FINDERS KEEPERS'. You should really go towards the light, the port for human spirits and live on their planet called Heaven."

Mad, Harley the human flesh colored spirit shot off toward the light port of the humans.

"That human spirit is not happy with you Benson." Moon Dance stated watching the spirit disappear into the distance.

"She or he, whichever the spirit is, can have this human vehicle back when I find another to travel in. For now, your safety and my watching your back door is more important than that human riding a hot pink motorcycle and dancing in a third rate, cross dresser's strip club."

"Your point is a valid one. Keep the body. Our survival supersedes the needs of a wimpy going nowhere human cross dresser. However, I wish you had chosen a more masculine body. It is hard for me to say 'I adore you' to that human vehicle you are traveling in without laughing."

"Your point has been noted. Should I choose another body in the future, I will try to choose a more masculine one." He stated laughing in his spirit form and then asked."Do you adore me?"

"You are growing on me, Benson."

"I am happy about that, Moon dance. I do adore you!"

"Exactly where are we, Benson?" Moon Dance asked as she turned around a couple of times in astral flight eyeing the teal colored universe and a sea of strangers in spirit form flying like angels in every which direction.

"We are between worlds, Moon Dance, where knowledge of future, present and past, dwells. We can go forward in time or back. We can go dancing in Chicago a hundred years ago, go horseback riding in Montana with the Indians of the old west, or travel to time square and experience what it will be like on New Year's Eve twenty years in the future. We can also go peep in on someone in the present moment we live. What would you like to do in our shared dream? If you wish to see the place humans call hell, we can go view it and you can go back and speak of a nightmare or we can shoot off into the human's Heaven and view it and go back speaking of the afterlife. Whatever you want is what this dream catcher experience will provide. We have traveled thru the dream catcher's web into the world of nightmares or pleasant dreams. The choice is ours."

"I wish two see two things and they might not be pleasant for you." She stated with an unsmiling face.

"I was a doctor of human minds, Moon Dance. There is nothing that surprises me. I know that one of your two wishes has to be to just take a tiny little peek at Gray Feather because the shattered pieces of your heart are still in love with him and won't let go. I am okay with that."

"You really are a special man, Jack Benson. What I want to see is whether he sleeps with Hissing Cat. If he does, he cannot have ever loved me. I will give my heart and memories of him to the hands of the nightmare web when I return thru the dream catcher. If he sleeps with her, I will know what a fool I was and am still."

"That is probably a wise choice, Moon Dance. Sooner or later, we all have to face our nightmares and he is yours. What is your second wish?

"I wish to travel to the land of Utah and see if the men who abandoned my tribe of women in the desert are still there or whether they managed to start their space crafts and make it home to the mother ship. I am hoping there are more Weelo on Earth besides just you and me. A pure Weelo tribe would be preferable to mating and bearing children by humans. In the young body of Sleeping Moon I could reproduce and form a new tribe."

"If you reproduce with anyone, it will be me. I claim my right. I am pure Weelo like you." Jack Benson replied.

"Your point is noted." She replied using his words and grinning at him. "I reserve the right to demand you find a new body before sleeping with me."

"Well, bow legs. I reserve the same right." He replied reaching over and tapping the end of her nose with the tip of one of his filmy blue fingers "Which do you wish to visit first, Gray Feather or your tribe in Utah?

"Gray Feather. I want my heart to go silent and beat no more for him. I cannot function still wanting him."

Jack Benson took Moon Dance by the hand and the two of them shot across the teal colored universe in the land of dreams and entered a strange Weelo planet dwelling that looked like it was in a zoo. It had glass walls on the exteriors of the structure and milk glass doors and walls in the center of the dwelling. They floated among the glass encased rooms. Spotting an open door on the milk glass hallway, they floated into a sleeping room. Hissing Cat was napping naked on a crystal bed with silk like sheets. It was a bed for two. However, Gray Feather was not in it.

"He has to be here." Moon Dance stated looking down at Hissing Cat with disgust. She didn't want to think about Gray Feather making love to Hissing Cat. He had never made love to her.

"Come on, Moon Dance. You have looked. Michael Gray Feather is not here or in her bed."

"There is one more milk glass door down the hall. I wish to look beyond it so I am satisfied. I want no doubts in my mind when we leave here. I also want to visit Pansy Sky Walker and see if he is in her bed."

Together, the pair of blue skinned spirit forms with crystal ears and nails floated down the cloudy milk glass hallway to the last room where the door was partially open. They floated in and Moon Dance instantly froze in spirit form. Gray Feather was there caring for three babies that looked to be about three months old. He had triplets. Each had black raven hair and only two eyes. The babies were human and not pure or half Weelo. Moon Dance began to cry in spirit form. As she did, a gust of fierce wind blew causing havoc with everything loose in the room. Jack Benson took Moon Dance's arm and forcibly pulled her out of the room quickly in fear for the babies. Moon Dance's sadness, anger, and tears were causing tornado or hurricane type winds. Weelo are capable of that.

Out in the hallway of the clear and milk glass dwelling, he spoke to Moon Dance in a firm voice. "Gray Feather has three children. You only get babies one way. It is time now to let him go! Look at the Weelo calendar on the wall. We have traveled a year into the future. You are seeing Gray Feather and Hissing Cat one year from today. They are married, Moon Dance. Gray Feather has babies and you know how human babies are conceived."

Thru a flood of blue filmy tears, Moon Dance replied. "First he gave a child to Pansy Sky Walker and now three in the future to my hair dresser. I am definitely an old fool. I used to make fun of the old men in our tribe who would chase young girls and marry them. When the old fools aged, the young girls would run off with the young bucks. Now, I laugh at myself. He tossed me aside like I was garbage."

"Come, I feel our bodies waking." Jack Benson stated being suddenly alarmed. We will have to do Utah during our next opportunity to enter the land of dreams and between worlds. We must go. Come!"

Taking Moon Dance's arm, he pulled her crying from the teal blue dream land of Planet Weelo and forced her to fly back across the universe of in-between worlds. Nervously, he then let her travel back thru the dream catcher first. As she floated thru the web of the dream catcher, she took her right filmy blue hand and tore out her blue heart that was in many shattered pieces. She then threw the pieces into the air for the many hands of the web to catch as she floated thru. The hands of the dream catcher scrambled to catch the pieces of her nightmare which was her love for Gray Feather.

Jack Benson panicked when he saw Moon Dance ripping out and throwing the pieces of her heart into the air for the web's hands to catch. He entered the web vicariously and started to grab for the pieces. He only managed to rescue one tiny piece of it when the hands grabbed him and threw him back into the in-between worlds. In shock, he rose from his fallen position in the Astral and prepared to try to float thru the web again. He had to make it past the hands and re-enter the body of Harley.

As he was rising and preparing to make another try at flying thru the web, an unexpected turn of events took place. Harley, the human spirit of the cross dresser from Las Vegas, appeared out of nowhere, shot thru the dream catcher, and instantly dove into his human vehicle before Jack Benson could stop him.

"No . . . !" shouted Jack Benson trying to float thru the dream catcher web whose hands threw him back into the in-between worlds again. Then he tried and tried to float thru the web with a tiny shattered fragment piece of Moon Dance's heart held tightly. The web's hands prevented him. He watched the cross dresser human spirit enter the human body known as Harley lying next to Moon Dance. Jack Benson was in a total panic. He held tightly to the fragment of her heart. Without that piece returned to her, she would never love again and he wanted her to love him. He would have to find another way back to her. He backed off from the web and put her tiny piece of shattered heart in his spirit form and pressed it like it was a piece of putty to his own heart for safe keeping.

In the room beyond the dream catcher, Moon Dance rested in her body being very tired from the adventure and being too sad concerning Gray Feather to face the world yet. The human spirit of Harley, however, quietly woke his body, rose from Moon Dance's bed, and tip toed out of Moon Dance's bedroom with the intention of exiting the ranch house and making his way back to Las Vegas and his former life. He wasn't taking any chances of a run in with Jack Benson who might find his way thru the dream catcher at any moment and beat the hell out of him. He was a tiny man and had to watch his back door. Just as he exited Sleeping Moon's bedroom, pulling the door quietly shut, he heard a familiar voice.

"Going somewhere?" Jerome Jeri Ann asked stepping out into the hallway from the guest bedroom blocking Harley's path.

Harley looked around, but couldn't see an escape route anywhere. The ranch house was unfamiliar to him and the only exit he could see was beyond Jerome thru the kitchen. There was light streaming from there.

"Get out of my way, Jerome. You are lucky I don't charge one of your rancher friends with kidnapping my body. I am not here by choice and I now intend to head back to Vegas and my new lover, Georgie." Harley stated in a high pitched voice imitating a woman.

"I want my mustang, my black book, and all of my designer clothes back that you stole from me at the hotel in Las Vegas. Those pink boots that you are wearing are mine as well as that sequined belt. Give them too me!" Jerome shouted forgetting he was a girl.

"They are mine and I am keeping them. You failed to pay the motel bill in Vegas and I had to work it off in the kitchen or go to jail. Georgie and I deserved better than that. After all, he was your dog walker too."

Jeri Ann Jerome made a mad dash for Harley grabbing at the pink sequined belt. Harley began to squeal and a cat fight ensued in the middle of the hallway. Both females, in male bodies, were pulling hair, biting, and scratching. Harley managed to get away and made a dash down the hall way and into the kitchen where Elkhorn was standing with a knife trimming some steaks. Elkhorn was shocked to see Harley's shirt half ripped off of him. He was then even more shocked to see Jeri Ann Jerome Mason slide into his kitchen and break for the back door chasing Harley. Had the two he/she men gone crazy? He walked to the kitchen door and eyed them as they engaged in a cat fight out back.

Then Harley managed to get away from Jerome and started sprinting away from the ranch house down the drive.

"Give me those boots and that belt." Jeri Ann Jerome yelled hot on Harley's heels.

Charlie Elkhorn had never seen two male cross dressers cat fight before. He grinned and stood in the kitchen doorway amused. Not interfering, he watched the pair physically attack each other once more half way down the back driveway. They screamed, pulled hair, and tore at each other's clothing. At one point, Jeri Ann Jerome had Harley on the ground and managed to pull one pink western cowgirl boot off of him. Then Harley managed to get away once more after causing a disaster to Jeri Ann Jerome's appearance.

"Oh . . . "Charlie Elkhorn gasped seeing Harley pull Jeri Ann Jerome's blouse half off. Then, a pair of falsies fell to the ground. Charlie muttered to himself. "Losing your falsies can't be a good thing when you are a pink she/he."

Then Harley managed to get a few steps ahead of Jeri Ann Jerome and started running down the lane toward the black top road beyond the ranch. He was running with one pink boot on faster than any border crosser Charlie Elkhorn had ever witnessed. Jeri Ann Jerome was hot on his heels chasing him, waving the falsies, and yelling obscenities.

"Border crossers . . . "Charlie Elkhorn muttered to himself suddenly having a light bulb moment. As he watched Jerome chasing Harley down the black top in front of the ranch, he had a brilliant idea. He picked up his cell phone off of the cabinet top. Then he rang the number for the border patrol telling them that two small Mexican border crossers, dressed in pink and purple western girl's clothes, were heading toward town and that he had watched them cross the Rio in a hot air balloon. No one could prove he hadn't seen a hot air balloon and that it was gone now. Plus, the purses, of the two he-she men were hanging on hooks by the back door. It didn't get any sweeter than that and it was payback time for all the misery they had caused him.

When the border patrol officer asked Charlie his name, he stated he was Night Hawk the owner of the Seven Moons Ranch.

Hanging up, he pulled a fresh cigar from his stash in the cabinet above the dishwasher and celebrated his sweet revenge. He was Arapaho and had won the Arapaho he-she war. Peace treaties were history.

CHAPTER ELEVEN

BONDING WITH SONG BIRD

When Moon Dance awoke in her bedroom after her adventure with Jack Benson thru the dream catcher, she was surprised to find him gone. Now, a month had passed and she wondered if her few hour journey thru the dream catcher with him was just fun and games on his part. Charlie Elkhorn had been delighted in telling her how Harley Jack Benson and Jeri Ann Jerome had slipped out the back door together, ran for the black top road in front of the ranch, and hitched a ride not returning. This destroyed what was left of Moon Dance's faith in men. She had believed Benson when he told her that he adored her. She had been a fool a second time and that was hard to swallow. Now, she needed to make plans for her future which was destined to be alone. She had chosen a quiet place to hide, sit, and think.

Moon Dance sat in the hall closet of the ranch house hiding from her brothers, the cook, the ranch hands, and grandmother Song Bird. It had been weeks and there had been no word from Jack Benson. She had to accept the fact that he had played some sort of game with her and then left with Jeri Ann Jerome to start a new life. He had kissed Jeri Ann. Moon Dance was mad at herself for waiting a month on Benson to return. He had fooled her just like Gray Feather.

The stress of dealing with her new family and her follies had taken a toll on Moon Dance. She wasn't feeling just right. She couldn't put her finger on what was wrong, but the body of Sleeping Moon was sluggish and slept a lot. A month ago, she had considered walking away from the ranch, hitching a ride, and starting a new life somewhere. However, when she woke up earlier, she realized that was not going to be possible. Her Sleeping Moon human body was not functioning like it had. Moon Dance wondered if it was slowly dying. She knew that Sleeping Moon had heart problems, but she didn't consider the fact that there might be other health complications. She now needed to go where babies were being conceived. She was sure that she was going to need a new body to travel in and very soon.

Sitting alone in the dark of the closet, she considered her predicament and what was best for the ailing body she was in. She had hoped to bond with Sleeping

Moon's Earth family and live out what was left of Sleeping Moon's life with them. However, she hadn't bonded with anyone on the ranch and she regretted big time incarnating in Sleeping Moon's body as well as not taking the Great Mother Ship home. She could have gone to live on one of the seven moons of Weelo as a hermit and never had to look at Gray Feather. She had made a decision in haste in a state of distraught emotions. She was Weelo and knew better. She should have manned her space craft, seen her tribe home, and refused Pansy and Gray Feather boarding privileges. She had that right. In her mind, she felt she had failed herself and her planet. Now, she must not make any more decisions based on emotions or ever love a human again. She no longer had a heart, so it was going to be easy. However, she didn't quite understand her attraction to Benson or why she wanted to wait for him the last month like an old fool. It was a small emotion she felt, but she did adore him. For some reason, she could swear she could feel his heart beating like it was hers. However, he had abandoned her while she slept not even saying goodbye. She had been twice a fool.

The dream catcher in Moon Dance's bedroom fascinated her and she considered going thru it again. She wanted to journey in sleep spirit form to Utah and then travel thru a dream catcher there and incarnate into a dying human body there somewhere. However, she feared the nightmare hands of the web. Now her human body was acting funny and she needed to reconsider everything including the feared dream catcher portal. She wished she had at least one Weelo tribe member to lean on. She felt so alone. Jeri Ann Jerome was lucky if she/he was in Benson's arms for Eternity.

As Moon Dance sat in the dark of the closet pretending it was a dark starry night, she considered her life back in the New Mexico desert with her tribe before Gray Feather. Somewhere in the last three to four years, she had lost who she was. The arrival of Gray Feather on the reservation was the beginning of her losing her identity. Suddenly, her thoughts were interrupted. She watched the door knob to the closet slowly turn and then the door open. Moon Dance closed her eyes knowing it had to be her two new crazy brothers and they were going to read her the riot act for something she was doing wrong. She took a deep breath. She needed this quiet time in the closet to sit and plan an escape.

The closet door opened and Moon Dance saw that it was Grandmother Song Bird peeping in. The elderly Indian grandmother then stepped inside, closed the door, and took a seat on the floor beside Moon Dance underneath the hanging coats.

"It is a good day to sit in a dark tee-pee hiding from White Eagle and Night Hawk. I am a Song Bird and in danger of getting my song taken from me. May I share your hiding place?"

"I gather White Eagle and Night Hawk are on your case about something?" Moon Dance asked pushing some shoe boxes out of the way so eighty-four year old Song Bird could be comfortable.

"I sang opera just as Night Hawk was about to make Indian magic with his Arapaho witch woman. He lost his concentration. Now, I am hiding from him to protect my song." Song Bird giggled.

Moon Dance smiled in the dark considering Grandmother Song Bird's words. In a moment or so, their eyes adjusted to the dark.

"You did what?" Moon Dance asked.

Night Hawk was about to sing a high note in the camper behind the barn when I hit a high note for him. I can shatter crystal when I need to. I have a fine voice."

"You are talking about hitting a high note like a white woman opera singer?"

"Yes, just at that special moment when Night Hawk was at his high point in lovemaking?"

"He is going to kill you, Grandmother Song Bird." Moon Dance giggled pulling her knees up in front of her. She then wrapped her arms around them and rested her chin on her knees. She felt so slow or under the weather. She couldn't pin point what was wrong with Sleeping Moon's body.

"Today is a great moment in my operatic career." Song Bird stated seriously and then giggled herself. "I am sure I ruined the moment for him and her."

Moon Dance bit her lip and then broke out into laughter. "Why would you do that? He is your grandson and in my opinion, he is aging. What if that lady friend is his last hope and you have doomed him to be an old bachelor?"

"It serves him right. Last year, when I had a gentleman friend call, Night Hawk threatened him with a shot gun if he ever showed up climbing thru my window again. White Eagle and Night Hawk made Tall Willow, my lover, ride naked in the back of a horse trailer all the way back to the Mason Ranch to embarrass him. I have not forgotten."

"They made your lover ride naked in the back of a horse trailer home?"

"Yes, and it was filled with horse crap."

"Did they have a reason?" Moon Dance asked fishing for details of the interesting story.

"They just wanted to spoil my high note!"

"It has been awhile since I had one. You are lucky if you have a Tall Willow. I am sorry that White Eagle and Night Hawk have in the past chosen to treat you so disrespectfully."

"I have made them many high notes sorry for their deed. White Eagle has lost seven girlfriends and Night Hawk's Arapaho Witch is afraid of me." Song Bird smirked in the dark closet. "Now you and I must join forces and spoil more of their high notes. Women must stick together. They would get rid of your lover too, if you had one. "

"They would not want me to have a male lover?"

"No, they don't want any extra men around to possibly inherit part of this ranch which they consider theirs. I had no intentions of marrying Tall Willow. I'm just a woman who needs a high note once in awhile. I am not dead yet. Tall Willow, the Mason's ranch hand, is one fine looking Arapaho. He is ninety, but can still make it thru my window."

"You have a ninety year old ranch hand lover named Tall Willow who makes his way over here at night and climbs thru your window instead of knocking on your front door?"

"Would you want your lover to knock and be given a horse trailer ride by White Eagle and Night Hawk?" Song Bird asked.

"I think I see where you are coming from." Moon Dance replied enjoying the conversation.

"John Mason, at Night Hawk's insistence, took my Tall Willow and put him in a nursing home for old Indians and cowboys declaring him to be senile. Today, I spoiled Night Hawk's high note in the camper out behind the barn and bunk-house. It was another chance for me to get revenge. I miss my Tall Willow and his Willow. If I am doing without high notes, I am making sure your brothers are doing so also."

Moon Dance snickered again and clapped her hand over her mouth as she heard a mad Night hawk walk the hallway yelling Grandmother Song Bird's name.

"Song Bird . . . I am going to stuff a croaking toad frog down your throat when I catch up with you." He shouted mad beyond the hall closet door looking for his grandmother.

It wasn't long till the two women heard Night Hawk slam the back screen door and leave cursing. They waited for a moment or so and then broke out in uncontrollable laughter. "You must teach me to hit a high note." Moon Dance snickered. I have not found a way to hold my own with my brothers since returning from the hospital."

"You cannot hit one sitting in a dark tee-pee. You only enter and hide in the tee-pee after you have hit the high note and got the best of them."

"I get your point." Moon Dance replied. "However, won't Night Hawk get even with you later in the day? We cannot stay in here forever."

"He will cool down. Later, I will brag about my high note raid to White Eagle. He will tease Night Hawk for days. Revenge is sweet." Song Bird stated grinning in the dark of the hall coat closet. "If you hide from White Eagle and Night Hawk like a timid rabbit, they own you. If you let them know that you are Apache and can raid their camps, steal their ponies, and declare war on their high notes, you own them. They will fear your Apache Warrior Spirit. Night Hawk will now fear bringing his lady friends home. He now fears me. I now own him." Song Bird replied.

"So you think I am hiding like a timid rabbit from my predators?" Moon Dance asked solemnly.

"I always strike Apache fear in the men in my tee- pee and never let them get the best of me or rule me. You must do the same if you wish to survive your brothers, the cook, ranch hands, and your past lovers. My bow and arrow is my high notes. I shoot and sing my arrows at inopportune moments raiding their love camps. They fear me so much that they promise me anything and everything to get me to smoke the peace pipe with them and cease my raids."

"So to survive, I must make them crazy so they will do anything to get me off their back."

"Yes. You must learn to shoot your own arrows and sing your own high notes. I dare you to tell Night Hawk you wish to accompany me to my singing lessons because you feel you have a gift for opera. It will drive him and your brother crazy thinking that you are going to walk in my Apache high note shoes."

"Walk in your shoes . . . , I get the point. When will Night Hawk see his lady friend again?"

"He always takes her to the travel trailer out by the bunkhouse on Saturday nights. Usually, they end up there about eleven after they have done some two stepping and drinking down at the Road Runner Club. Night Hawk's lady friend is very loud with her high love note. That is when you or I should shoot our arrow, sing our high note, and then run like Hell."

"Running is important?" Moon Dance asked enjoying Song Bird's tale.

"You can hang around if you are into cat fights and want Night Hawk's witch woman to pull your hair out by the roots. I prefer raiding parties where I steal their ponies and then ride away quickly into the night."

"That is another good point. I think I am the raiding party type as well."

"A couple of times, I have brought them out of the bunk house chasing me, throwing shoes, and calling me an evil kachina. They are always barefoot and never catch me. Night Hawk is a tender foot."

"You have let me see my brother, Night Hawk, in a whole new light." Moon Dance giggled again. "I have not till now pictured him as a hop around, barefoot frog on gravel throwing shoes and boots because his pony has been stolen right out from under his nose."

"He would have made a poor warrior if he had been born back in the seventeen and eighteen hundreds. His tender feet would have gotten him killed running from his tee-pee during a raid. He runs across gravel and rocks like a girl. Now, White Eagle is another story. You have to have your running shoes on when hitting a high note for him. He is a fierce warrior and has captured me and tanned my backside a couple of times."

"White Eagle has smacked your backside?" Moon Dance asked in shock eyeing the petite grandmother wearing long white braids

"He whacked my backside good three months ago. I crept into his bedroom and dribbled honey on him and his lady friend while they slept in bare butts. I had a quart jar of worker honey bees with me and was opening the container knowing the bees would go for the honey on his lady friend's bare backside. Just as I was opening the jar of bees, a breeze from an open window slammed his bedroom door shut. It sticks sometimes. I had to make a run for his bedroom window to get out and he caught me. His feet and body were sticky with the honey. As he was jumping from his bed and running to catch me, he excited some of the bees who might have all been girl bees. They found the sight of his bare butt exciting and they really buzzed...The boy worker bees were not happy and they declared war on his backside. He got me. The bees got him and his naked honey coated lady friend. She doesn't come around anymore. She was not very thankful for the bees or the free honey."

"I wish I had been there. I would have held the door open for you on the raid." Moon Dance laughed loving the story.

"He was one mad Indian and instantly declared war on me. My backside got his arrow arms. I am looking for a chance to make another raid on his camp. Currently, he takes his ladies to motel rooms. He is afraid of me. I own him, even if he did smack my backside." Song Bird stated grinning. "If you want to tease him, call him Honey Butt."

"I have just become a great admirer of you, Grandmother Song Bird. I once was a warrior. However, a great chief named Gray Feather raided my camp and stole from me all of my high notes. Now, I will reclaim them and once again lead my tribe and survive. I am a great warrior, not a timid rabbit and God forbid if I ever catch White Eagle whacking your backside again. He will find Rattlesnakes in his bed. They are part of my high notes."

"Own him, Moon Dance. Tell him about the snakes in his bed. It will be good magic for you and me." Grandmother Moon Dance laughed.

"I swear to you I will before the day is over. I am tired of men walking on me and I am not going to let them disrespect you either."

"Welcome to my tribe, Moon Dance. I am getting old and I need a new young warrior to lead my Apache raids. We will be feared by the tribe of White Eagle, Night Hawk, and Elkhorn. We the Apache will make new night raids and dance around the campfire telling of our victories. They hate it when we go to powwows and I tell of my raids around the campfires. They do not like it known that they run from an Apache woman and her magic high note."

"I am with you, Song Bird. When I leave this closet, I will go straight to White Eagle and declare my intentions with the Rattlesnakes and throw my spear covered with war feathers at his feet."

"I need you Sleeping Moon. The tribe needs you. I personally do not have another woman to share my warpath moments of victory with. Could we be friends? I need a woman warrior to night hunt with who can sing opera when needed."

"I need you for a friend way more than you need me, Grandmother Song Bird. Would it be too much for you to call me Moon Dance? I don't see myself as Sleeping Moon. I will dance across the night sky and shoot my arrows."

"I will call you Moon Dance if you will drop the grandmother and call me Song Bird. Grandmother makes me sound really old and I do not see myself that way."

"Song Bird it is. Also, why don't we make our first raid on Charlie Elkhorn's kitchen and steal all of his cigar peace pipes. I discovered his secret hiding place on the top shelf above the dishwasher. I was looking for chocolate. If you watch our ponies, I will raid his camp and steal his magic. He is addicted to his cigars and will have a Nicotine fit. He will go crazy without them and have to drive to town for more. It would be a great raid that we can tell at the fall campfire when all of the other tribal nations come to call and share."

"A cigar raid it is. Also, Moon dance, I know that you are not Sleeping Moon. I saw her spirit leave the night she was on the operating table. She whispered in my ear and in my dreams afterwards that she was sending me a new tribe member to live in her body. That is okay with me. I know you must be a Kachina spirit, a witch like the one that lives down by the Rio Grande that Night Hawk sees."

"I am sort of a witch, Song Bird. I was a medicine woman on a reservation in New Mexico. I killed myself with a rattlesnake bite and exited my body which was seventy some years old. I was floating about the hospital where your granddaughter was having surgery looking for a body to enter. I was there when your granddaughter's spirit left her body and floated up to where I was. I asked her if I could enter and use her body if she was finished with it. She said I could have it because she was going home to the Great White Spirit. I have been winging it here as they say. I have no memories of you." She stated being honest with Song Bird.

"I like you Moon Dance. No one need know your secret but me. Having a witch on my side is good magic. Night Hawk has one."

"Thank you Song bird. I am trying to find myself and who I am in this family. Until now, you have all scared the hell out of me. I am not use to pranksters. Before coming here, I was the provider for my tribe. I had ten women and one child to feed every day with no men to help us. I had to catch at least three rattlers every day for our meat. This ranch is not a place of survival. I am at lost as how to fit in here. You have money, food, and grandsons who provide for you. You go to white doctors and have no need of a medicine woman's magic."

"I will help you fit in, if you will help me with my problem. You being a witch, you may be able to solve my mystery. There has been humming in the third floor loft of the barn ever since my newlywed husband and I built it over sixty-five years ago. You are a kachina. You can see and hear between worlds. I need your eyes and ears. I think the humming is the voice of aliens."

Moon Dance grinned knowing that she herself was one. "I will be your eyes and now, I am curious about the humming myself. I also have heard it when I walk the desert near the barn."

"I have been told that I am crazy. I need you to help me prove that I am not."

"I am a Kachina; I will not give up till I solve your mystery."

"Just be careful. Sometimes the hummers take people. They took my grandson's mother. She came up missing about fifteen years ago. There was humming. I heard her scream somewhere in the desert near the barn. Tall Willow heard it. He was here that night with me in my bedroom. We found no body."

"I will be careful. You watch my backside and I will watch yours. You and I are now members of the same Apache, kachina tribe. We will be a force to deal with and I will catch your hummer. However, for now, we are going on an Apache raid starting in Elkhorn's kitchen. That box of cigars on his high shelf in the kitchen is ours. I have a live frog in my pocket that I caught down on the bank of the Rio. I am going to send to Charlie Elkhorn and the boys a message not to mess with me. Not only will I leave the live frog in place of the cigars, I will also take an ink pen and draw a quick Rattlesnake in the bottom of his empty cigar box. I am going to shoot my first arrow and instill a little fear. We get the cigars and Charlie gets a warning. I am no longer a Weelo medicine woman who had her magic stolen from her; I am now an Apache kachina witch. I intend to make the men in our world shake in their boots as I cast my spells. Night Hawk's witch's magic will pale in comparison to mine.

"I am pleased, Moon Dance. Could you use your magic to bring Tall Willow back to me?

"I will do my best to draw Tall Willow back to you. Do you think there might be a tall Willow out there for me somewhere?"

"There is a Tall Willow in love with you, but you don't see him." Song Bird replied. "Charlie Elkhorn is trying to get your attention."

"Charlie Elkhorn likes me? " Moon Dance questioned and then added laughing, "He may not be so interested in being my Tall Willow once he finds my magic, kachina frog and the snake drawing in his cigar box."

Song Bird laughed. "I think that is what he finds so attractive about you. You don't take any crap off of him. That frog and Rattlesnake drawing will be a form of love note, to him."

CHAPTER TWELVE

THE APACHE RAIDS

R aiding the kitchen was not a problem. The two new raiding party buddies waited quietly in the hallway off the kitchen until Charlie Elkhorn had a Mother Nature call. Then, they quickly entered his kitchen. Song Bird acted as the lookout or pony rein holder. Moon Dance retrieved the box of cigars from the cabinet above the dishwasher and then scooped up its content of a dozen or more stogies and stuck them into the pocket of her long Navajo type cotton skirt. She then took a pen from her pocket and drew a quick snake in the bottom of the cigar box and then put in the small frog from her pocket. Quickly she closed the lid and put it back on the shelf above the dishwasher.

"Hurry . . . !" Song Bird whispered after hearing the sound of a toilet flushing.

Moon Dance had gone to great effort to catch the little green frog down by the Rio. She had been carrying it around all day in her pocket looking for a way to get back at Elkhorn for putting a plastic one in the bottom of her oatmeal bowl at breakfast. She was pleased with herself. It was an easy raid. She motioned for Song Bird to head for the back door. Hearing the sound of footsteps, they exited quickly the ranch house kitchen and ran for the barn. Moon Dance was sure that Charlie would want a cigar, possibly just before serving dinner. She would have loved to see him open the box, jump around mad, and curse possibly when he opened the cigar box. However, she felt it was not in her and Song Bird's best interest.

Once inside the barn, Moon Dance looked at Song Bird and went to giggling."I haven't had this much fun in years. Charlie Elkhorn is going to be one mad Indian when he finds his cigars have been lost to an Apache raiding party. Now what are we going to do with our plunder? We can't hide them in the house, he will find them?"

"Good thinking, Chief Moon Dance. We are at war and need a safe place along the Rio to water our ponies, camp, and hide our plunder. Follow me! On the third floor loft of this barn is a wooden locker that was once used by our first ranch hand. He slept up there till the hummers frightened him off. He said a great light shown in the top of the barn and purple skinned beings tried to snatch him. My husband said he was a drunk and we were better off without him. I now believe his story."

"Have you seen purple skinned aliens?" Moon Dance asked knowing that Sleeping Moon had been one. Perhaps there were more.

"None of our hands will sleep up there. They say the barn is inhabited by a Kachina. My husband had to build a bunkhouse in order to keep help. Now, only I go up there. One day, I will catch one of the purple skinned Kachina, shoot him like a deer, and bring him down so everyone will not think I am crazy. We will use the first ranch hand's wooden locker to hide the treasures of our raids. Do you have your handgun, Moon Dance?"

"Yes, I do. White Eagle insisted I carry it in my skirt pocket." Moon Dance stated pulling the top out so Song Bird could see it. "Lead the way."

Song Bird walked past horse stalls to the back of the barn and began to climb a roughly built, straight up wooden ladder that went all the way up to the third floor hay loft.

Moon Dance followed suit and held tightly to the rough wooden ladder following and climbing upward behind Song Bird. This was a first for her. In the New Mexico desert, in her last life, there were no trees or anything to climb. She didn't fear for herself as she climbed, but she was concerned about her eighty-four year old raiding friend. To her surprise, the ascent was no problem. Song Bird moved liked a twenty year old climbing upward.

Reaching the second floor hay loft, they stepped off into it briefly. Song Bird seemed to be listening for something. Moon Dance listened also. Perhaps, Charlie Elkhorn was what she was listening for. Moon Dance did not hear Charlie, but she did hear a strange, faint, humming noise. Then, Song Bird stepped back onto the ladder and continued to climb upwards. Moon Dance followed her. As they were nearing the top of the ladder and the third floor loft, Moon Dance noticed that the strange humming was louder.

"What is that humming?" She asked as they stepped off into the third floor loft.

"Aliens . . . They hum when they are speaking to you. I am glad someone hears it besides me. My dead husband could not hear it."

Amused, Moon Dance replied. "The ranch has aliens hiding up here in the third floor barn loft?" It sounded to her more like the hum of a motor, possibly a refrigerator kicking on.

"Aliens have lived up here since my dead husband and I built the barn when we were first married. They are hummers."

"Do you know what the humming aliens are saying to you?" Moon Dance asked going along with Song Bird. The humming had to come from some piece of electrical equipment somewhere.

"No. They hum, I hit high notes, and you whistle. I have heard you whistle when you walk out into the desert. It is your special sound. The aliens hum. It is their special sound. They try to drive me crazy with it just like I try to drive Night Hawk crazy with my high note. They come, they hum, and they take things like our cigars. However, I am never able to catch them. You will see. They will raid our secret plunder hiding spot and smoke our cigars."

Moon Dance grinned thinking that Song Bird possibly intended to sneak up to the loft later and smoke one. She would go along with her. After all, she was eighty-four. "So, have you ever seen one of the hummers?"

"No, but I have tried to sterilize one."

"Sterilize . . . I don't understand . . ."

"If aliens mate with you, you have ugly children with three eyes and maybe three extra big toes." She stated. "If I manage to sterilize the alien before he gets to me, I can enjoy his raid without having to worry about babies. A girl can't be too choosey at my age. I look forward to raids."

Moon Dance went to laughing and snickering. "And just how do you sterilize an alien? I don't think one would submit to it willingly."

"I keep a bucket filled with water by the barn door. I listen for the hum. When I hear the humming start, I balance the bucket of water on top of the barn door after pouring in a half gallon of bleach in it. If an alien opens the barn door and walks in, the bucket of bleach water falls on him drenching him. He is sterilized just like the clothes in my washer and I never get pregnant."

Moon Dance broke out in uncontrollable snickering and laughter. She had not expected the pregnant part of the story to pop out of eighty-four year old Song Bird's mouth. She sat down on the loft floor and laughed till her eyes were filled with tears. Drying them on the tail of her long, turquoise blue Navajo skirt, she bit her lip and then continued their conversation.

"And just how many times have you slept with aliens, Song bird, and not got pregnant?"

"Not many. Usually, the aliens are very angry after being doused with bleach. I have got away most of the time."

"I can't imagine why they would be angry." Moon Dance replied biting her lip and then tuning in once more to the humming in the loft. She couldn't figure out where it was coming from. It seemed to come from the area of the third floor hay loading window, but she couldn't see anything that could make the noise. All that existed, up on the third floor, was hay and unfinished, gray, aging, stud walls. There was no electricity up there, so it couldn't be a radio or other piece of electrical equipment. She was intrigued. "Will one of these hummers be arriving soon?"

"He will come tonight and smoke our cigars. When the humming starts, I can expect to have an encounter between the ten o'clock news and midnight"

"Will we be raiding the Hummer's camp tonight and giving one of them the bleach treatment? We are a tribe now. Will you or I sleep with this one?" She asked biting her lip and trying not to laugh at the old woman who was probably sliding into a touch of dementia.

"He will come tonight after ten thirty, after the news. The hummer is very predictable. He will enter the barn, raid our box of cigars, and hum till after midnight. He then will leave. I have to catch him by the door entering, if I wish to sleep with him. A couple of times, I have caught ranch hands by mistake. They are no fun to sleep with. They always smell like horses and cattle."

Moon Dance broke out laughing again.

"Is tonight a good night to sterilize an alien ranch hand? I am a little lonely." Moon Dance asked going along with Song Bird's possible fantasy.

"We must leave now, Moon Dance. I hear and recognize the hum. If we are discovered, the ugly three eyed aliens might snatch us off this loft to never be seen again. They got your brothers' mother. Store our cigars quickly over there in that wooden foot locker. It is not safe for us here. I have no bleach with me."

Moon Dance did as she was told. Then, she and Song Bird climbed down. The hum was definitely on the third floor. It lessened as they descended the ladder.

Song Bird and Moon Dance hid out till dinner time playing cards in the old camper trailer behind the barn and bunk house to stay clear of Charlie Elkhorn.

Night Hawk often held poker games in the old travel trailer with his rancher friends. He never entertained his poker buddies in the ranch house for fear of Song Bird pulling a prank of some sort. She was ruthless in what she could think of to pull. It didn't matter whether the unsuspecting guest was male or female. If she didn't consider them part of her fantasy Apache tribe, they were fair game to raid.

While playing cards with Song Bird, Moon Dance considered what the grandmother had said about the three eyed Aliens mating with humans. She herself had mated many times down thru the centuries in an effort to survive and produce babies for her fellow Weelo to incarnate in. All Weelo had three eyes when they stepped from their human bodies. She wondered if Song Bird had somehow encountered a Weelo like herself who possibly had just unzipped and discarded his human form. She wondered if the witch across the river, the one that Night Hawk was supposedly dating, was a Weelo. Rumor was that she had a third eye in her forehead. Then she wondered about Tall Willow, Song Bird's lover. Could he possibly be Weelo? Maybe there were others like her in and around the ranch who had missed rescue.

Five minutes before dinner, Moon Dance and Song Bird slipped into the ranch house and took their place at the dinner table where Night Hawk and White Feather were already seated grinning. Charlie Elkhorn busied himself carrying plates of food from the kitchen and placing them in front of everyone. When he placed plates in front of Moon Dance and Song Bird, there was one tiny deep fried frog leg on each plate along with a baked potato. The men all got steaks. It was a declaration of war on Charlie Elkhorn's part who was Arapaho. Night Hawk and White Eagle never said a word. However, their smirk grins said it all. They welcomed war with the women. The deep fried frog legs were their declaration of war.

When Charlie Elkhorn sat down at the table, he pulled out a cigar from his pocket and laid it next to his dinner plate. Night Hawk and White Eagle did the same. Nothing else was said.

Later that evening, the women found all of their white bras, underwear, and socks died frog green. Then later in the week, when they were shampooing, their hair turned a hideous shade of green, especially eighty-four year old Song Bird's waist length white hair. Charlie Elkhorn had added green food coloring to their Green Apple Shampoo.

The Apache tribe retaliated by rubbing Charlie Elkhorn's toilet seat with Poison Ivy leaves. He couldn't sit down for a week.

Night Hawk and White Eagle, fearing the women, then cleaned their toilet seats every time they used them after discovering what Charlie Elkhorn was affected with.

The Apache women tribe was feared and had the Arapaho shaking in their boots. Night Hawk and White Eagle did not miss out on the poison Ivy raid. Song Bird ground up some of the leaves and sprinkled it in their underwear drawer. They broke out and abandoned wearing underwear. The two Apache women owned the men's fear. War was good!

CHAPTER THIRTEEN

WHITE EAGLE'S BLOOD OATH

Another month passed. Moon Dance had accompanied Song Bird on several adventures to the barn to catch aliens humming with no luck. Song Bird was fun and had lots of stories to tell including ones about the Kachina witch with three eyes that lived down by the river, told fortunes, made love potions, and bewitched men including Night Hawk. Moon dance planned to call on the Kachina witch as soon as she had an opportunity. She wanted to see if Night Hawk's witch did have three eyes like the Weelo and Plutonian. She was sure that the witch had to have some sort of birth defect or scar on her forehead. However, Song Bird's mention of ugly three eyed children and the witch's third eye had roused her curiosity.

Moon Dance and Song Bird had been relentless the past month in their raids of Charlie Elkhorn's kitchen and living quarters off of the kitchen. Today, they planned to remove his dishwasher door and hide it. Giving Charlie dishwater hands for a day or so should constitute a nice little raid. Plus, they were going to put a vial of blue food coloring in his bottle of dish liquid. He would have blue hands after hand washing dishes. The night before, he had short sheeted their beds and removed all of the extra linens from the hall closet. An Apache never lets a night raid go without a payback raid. The dishwasher door was their focus. Moon dance was ready, having a screw driver in her skirt pocket.

It was mid-afternoon. Lunch was over and Charlie Elkhorn was thru with the mid-day clean up. Moon Dance and Song Bird tip-toed into the kitchen. They had heard Charlie Elkhorn leave by the back door, get in his pickup truck, and drive down the lane. It was supermarket day. The two women turned and grinned at each other. This raid was going to be an easy one. Song Bird stayed at the door, just in case, as a lookout. Moon Dance removed the door and then made her way to the kitchen door carrying the clumsy object and stood beside Song Bird. They would hide it on the back porch behind a huge square metal barbecue when there were no ranch hands looking their way. They didn't see anyone stirring outside, so they prepared to open the back door and exit when a raiding party of the Arapaho snuck up behind them. White Eagle stepped quietly out of the side pantry where the freezer was. He crept up behind the two and then poked them both in the ribs yelling, "I got you. I just knifed you! You are either dead or my hostage now."

Not expecting the rib jab, Moon Dance screamed and turned toward her attacker. In fright, she dropped the dishwasher door on White Eagle's bare socked foot. Shoes were not worn inside the ranch house. White Eagle yelled and began to dance around saying a choice word or two. Song Bird spun around from her lookout position to face their enemy. The two Apache women had been totally surprised. She then screamed like a kachina letting every high note she could hit out of her mouth. White Eagle regained his composure and quickly grabbed Moon Dance securing her in his arms and then tickled the Hell out of her ribs with his fingers to hear her squeal and giggle. When she was begging for mercy, he grabbed Song Bird and secured her in his arms and started tickling her.

"You are now prisoners of the Arapaho." White Eagle shouted laughing." I have caught the raiders of Charlie Elkhorn's kitchen camp. I am the victor. The Arapaho reigns."

"You have had it, White Eagle. You just wait till I get over my laughing and my high note is back. Your love life will get my next raid." Song Bird shouted and then giggled and squealed as White Eagle went for her ribs tickling her relentlessly. In between bouts of squealing and giggling, she yelled."Your Arapaho torture will be revenged! Your love life is mine!"

"I have captured your raiding party and I am the victor and one smart Arapaho." He yelled laughing at his grandmother's giggling and squealing. He loved her dearly.

"You may have captured me, but I can sing my high note outside your teepee till you send me back to the Apache tribe." She shouted between bouts of tickling and giggling.

"I don't bring my lady companions home to my ranch house tee-pee at night anymore. I take my ladies to the lodge in the sky called the Rio Inn. It is a well guarded Arapaho camp. You will not find high note singing kachina like you there."

"No camp is too guarded for me, not even the Rio Inn!" Song Bird shouted back as he continued to tease her with tickling fingers."Have you forgotten that I am an Apache Song Bird with fierce high notes and have a driver who takes me to town?"

"I have not forgotten that you are an Apache Kachina Song Bird Witch. I well remember your last high note raid. It cost me one wild . . . woman. Now you are my wild woman!" He laughed wiggling his fingers.

"I am not a wild woman. I am a Song bird. You just wait! A Song Bird's revenge on you will be sweet high notes of music. One high note for every time you have tickled me should be a fair return raid."

"I am one smart Arapaho. I know what a motel room door lock is. Only Night Hawk still brings his women home to the trailer behind the barn. His Kachina witch with three eyes is coming tonight. I dare you to tangle with her. She is capable of putting a spell on you. She just might turn you into an ugly old duck that can only quack. Ducks cannot hit high notes."

"The three- eyed Witch will be here tonight?" Moon Dance asked excitedly.

White Eagle turned to Moon Dance, grabbed her again, and started to tickle her with no mercy. She fought him off with her hands. He backed up grinning.

"I have captured a Sleeping Moon that I am going to offer to the witch as payment for a love potion for me and my gal Sal. Perhaps, Night Hawk's Witch will turn you into a frog and Charlie Elkhorn can French- fry you and serve you for dinner. I think I might enjoy a mess of bow legged frog legs." He laughed wiggling his fingers at her.

Moon Dance lunged at him and went for his underarms. He immediately gave up his attack of tickling to try to get Moon Dance's hands away from his underarms. That was his tickle spot.

"Torture him, Moon Dance, we are fierce warriors and we will escape his captivity after we steal all of his laughter."

Then both women tore into White Eagle going for his underarms. He ended up in the floor wrestling the two women to get them off of him and away from his underarms. He was crazy about his sister and grandmother and let them win. He went to begging for mercy. The two women gave him one last good tickling to hear him squeal. Then they backed off.

"You are the victor, Grandmother Song Bird." He said getting up from the kitchen floor and helping her to her feet. Then he gave Moon Dance a hand.

Song Bird grinned from ear to ear. She reached up and pinched White Eagle's cheek affectionately. "It takes a smart Arapaho to know when to surrender. You now belong to two fierce Apache women. We own you and your laughter."

"I am your slave till the Arapaho steal me back." White Eagle replied amused with the two of them."Do I now sleep in your Tee-pee or Sleeping Moon's? I will get my sleeping bag and spread it there except on Saturday night when I sleep at the Rio Inn with a high note cawing raven named Sal. She owns my Saturday nights."

"We are going to let you live to ride your pony another day, White Eagle. Renting a motel room tee-pee is a well thought out Arapaho move. I tip my high note to you in respect. However, since the Rio Inn is the only motel in the next town, your new Saturday night camp has been discovered by the Apache and may be raided. Beware! I can still drive and ride a horse if necessary."

"Damn it!" White Eagle stated suddenly straight faced. "You wouldn't really raid my motel room, would you? I kind of like that waitress Sal that I am seeing."

"The Apache never lay their bows and arrows down till they are the victors. You belong to us, not the white woman. Perhaps we will take cawing Sal captive."

White Eagle put his arm around both of the women and kissed them both on the tops of their heads. Then he dropped the motel subject and asked. "What are you and Sleeping Moon doing today other than driving Charlie crazy by taking his dishwasher door?"

"To begin with, I have renamed Sleeping Moon. She is now Moon Dance. When Sleeping Moon was born ill, I expected her to die within hours. I named her Sleeping Moon because I expected her to sleep in death under the stars before midnight. She has defied death. She is a dancer who chooses Rattle snakes for partners. From this day forward, she is Moon Dance and you will call her by her new name. If you don't, I will sign you up for ball room dancing as her partner. Her companions, Jeri Ann Jerome and Harley, are gone. They ran off together. Charlie Elkhorn has two left feet. Moon Dance needs a cha-cha partner. I am sure that Chief Night Hawk of the Arapaho would agree to send you to be Moon Dance's partner for the cha-cha-cha. I am sure he would see the beauty of you learning to sissy white man dance.

"You wouldn't?" White Eagle gasped. I am a western shirt, two step man, not a tux and sissy shoes one."

"Tell your sister what you will call her from this day forward."

"Moon Dance is a good name and fitting for my Apache sister. I do hope she sticks to campfire dancing with me. She can cha-cha-cha the hell out of one of the ranch hands on our payroll."

"I think we have come to a reasonable understanding." Song Bird stated grinning from ear to ear. "What do you think, Moon Dance?"

"I will cha-cha-cha with a ranch hand or perhaps Charlie Elkhorn. I think it would be a great victory on our part to make him cha-cha-cha with me. He did fill my shoes last week with chocolate syrup while I slept in an Arapaho raid on my bedroom camp."

"Oh . . . "Song Bird stated in a drawn out expression. "Charlie Elkhorn is a no nonsense Arapaho who only does the rain dance at powwows. I like the idea of being able to tell the great tale of how the Great Charlie Elkhorn took sissy dance lessons. All of his Arapaho brothers will snort, belly laugh, and rib him. That would be a great raid on his dignity. Are you willing Moon Dance?"

"I am willing. Last week I was not happy to have chocolate feet. I think paying him back by forcing his feet and boots to cha-cha-cha with me would be an appropriate raid of revenge." Moon Dance replied biting her lip. Her new family lived to prank each other.

"It is settled! Charlie Elkhorn will be Moon Dance's cha-cha-cha partner and drive her to lessons." Song Bird stated grinning. "He may also take you to dinner if he wishes." She added grinning at Moon Dance.

"I am going to love this one," White Eagle laughed. "What do you mean he can take my sister to dinner? He hasn't asked me or Night Hawk about it."

"Do you wish them to cha-cha-cha, use up all of their foot magic, and then not return home because they have starved to death on the way?" Song Bird asked staring White Eagle in the eye.

"Your point is taken. However, I will have a talk with Charlie Elkhorn. You and I both know Moon Dance is a . . . "White Eagle stated not finishing his sentence because he suddenly saw that his sister's eyes were the wrong color. He didn't know what to make of it.

"You belong to our tribe now. I am sure the Arapaho will try soon to steal you back. For now, you must join Moon Dance and me on our next raid and hold the reins of our ponies."

White Eagle grinned at the two women he adored. "I happen to know that Night Hawk and the Three Eyed witch are going to be making a little magic in the old pickup camper out back of the bunk house in about a half hour. Are the two of you in for a few high notes and some trailer shaking?"

"Do we trust our new captor who will hold our pony's reins?" Moon Dance asked eyeing Song Bird. "Does he speak with a forked tongue?"

"If he does, I can always shoot his high note arrow with my pistol. There would be no reason for him then to have a tee-pee at the Rio Inn. He would be a girl and no maiden would want him." Song Bird replied grinning from ear to ear at her grandson who she loved to tease.

"I swear allegiance!" White Eagle quickly retorted raising his hand. He had a date; the first in a long time, for Saturday night and he didn't want his grandmother showing up with her high note and pop gun spoiling it.

"You answered too quickly, White Eagle." Song Bird stated. "Perhaps Moon Dance is right and your tongue speaks what we want to hear. You must take a blood oath of allegiance to us."

"Are you saying what I think you are saying?" White Eagle asked solemn faced eyeing his grandmother.

"You are our captive and possibly a traitor snitch and spy. Swear your allegiance to Moon Dance and me with a blood oath."

"You know that I faint at the sight of blood. We do not do blood oaths. We made that peace treaty when we were teens. Do you want me to go to bed and stay there for the rest of the day? Blood oaths make me sicker than a horse."

Moon Dance looked at him strangely smirking. He saw it and winked at her when the grandmother wasn't looking. Then she watched Song Bird walk over to the kitchen counter and pull a sharp knife from its wooden holder.

"Stick out your hand, White Eagle. You are a captor and treaties do not apply when there is a war raging. We are at war with Chief Elkhorn and Night Hawk. You will swear a blood oath of allegiance to us or die a painful death of us tickling your underarms till you give up your laughing spirit and go to meet our Great White Catholic Mother in the sky."

"Please, Grandmother Song Bird, I have never handled blood oaths well." White Eagle whined.

"Stick your hand out first Moon Dance and shame him. Show this wimpy little Arapaho what a fearless warrior you are."

Moon Dance took a deep breath and held out her hand. Song Bird took the sharp knife and gave her hand a little quick poke making it bleed. She could see White Eagle starting to turn a funny shade of color. He was holding his breath. As her hand bled, she grinned watching his reaction. If he didn't breathe soon, he was going to pass out. Then she realized he intended to please Song Bird.

"Stick your hand out now, White Eagle!" demanded Song Bird.

White Eagle did as he was told, staring at his sister and holding his breath. Then Song Bird took the knife and gave a quick little knife point prick of a stick to his hand causing it to bleed. White Eagle flinched. Then Song Bird put White Eagle's and Moon Dance's bleeding hands together with their blood mixing. Leaving them standing there with their bloody hands joined, she stepped over to the kitchen cabinet and grabbed a tea towel from a rack and returned to the pair. She then tied their hands together with it.

"You and Moon Dance are blood brothers for life and this oath stands before the Great Spirit. Say blood brothers for life, Moon Dance." Song Bird Instructed.

"I am your Apache blood brother for life!" Moon Dance stated eyeing White Eagle who was still holding his breath. He looked really funny.

"Say it, White Eagle!" Song Bird stated to the ashen man.

"I . . . I . . . I am your blood brother for . . . "he managed to get out and then fainted, pulling Moon Dance to the floor on top of him because their hands were tied together.

Song bird broke out in laughter seeing Moon Dance sprawled on top of fainted White Eagle. She then stooped over and untied the tea towel and helped a giggling, snickering Moon Dance to her feet.

"I didn't exactly expect that!" Moon Dance laughed with tears in her eyes.

"He is one of us now. However, he is going to be one wimp should we ever have to go on a serious raid with our bows and arrows. He definitely is not a killer. Did you know we have to send our animals to a processing plant to have them killed and butchered? White eagle has never been able to wring a chicken's neck, much less kill a deer to put in our freezer. It is a good thing I like steak and bacon." Song Bird added turning to return the bloody knife to the sink for washing.

With their backs turned to White Eagle briefly, they didn't see him open one eye slightly peeping at them. He was also biting his lip to keep from laughing. He loved those two crazy women with all of his heart and if they wanted to play Indian raid for the day, that was alright with him. At least the women in his family weren't wimpy pig squealers. They were fun. He quickly closed his eyes and pretended to be passed out. It was a good ploy for the moment, till he figured out what they were up to. All was fair in love, Indian raids, and war. However, he had a problem. When his grandmother had tied his hand to Moon Dance's and their blood mixed he had felt a strange coldness flow thru his veins from her. Also, He felt pain as though she was shattered somehow. He didn't know quite what to make of it. He had taken her sadness in him and let his heart beat for the two of them. He wondered if he had suddenly become psychic like the three eyed witch down by the Rio. It was an eerie supernatural experience for him.

Laying on the cold, red tiled, ranch house kitchen floor; White Eagle thought about when he, Night Hawk, and Sleeping Moon had been elementary age. One weekend, they divided into two Indian tribes and had Indian raids and wars inside the barn. It had been raining and they could not go outside to play. Song Bird, his mother, and Sleeping Moon became the Apache tribe. He, Night Hawk and their one ranch hand back then had become the Arapaho tribe. It was such a memorable, fun day that they had continued the tribal wars ever since then. Raiding and pulling pranks had become a life time, family game.

The two tribes had varied in size according to who was willing to join them. Charlie Elkhorn after accepting the position of cook and companion for Song Bird joined the Arapaho after Song Bird had high noted him a couple of times when he had a lady friend in his quarters for the night. The women were down to two members. The family's mother had disappeared in the desert and was presumed dead. Jeri Ann Jerome and Harley would probably have joined the Apache women, had they stuck around. The bunk house boys were Arapaho, but occasionally let themselves get captured in exchange for one of Song Bird's Lemon Meringue pies. Some families participated in sports. White Eagle's family waged raids and Indian wars.

"We do have a problem!" Moon Dance snickered walking over to the kitchen sink and running some cool tap water over her bloody hand. Then she wet a dish towel with cold water and returned to White Eagle. She stooped down and started to wash his fake fainted face with the cold water causing him to come to. Moon Dance sat down on the floor with White Eagle and picked up his hand. For the first time, she appreciated who he was. He was a gentle man who couldn't kill an animal much less a man. He was also willing to play games with his grandmother and let her win. She liked that. His six foot two macho muscled frame was deceiving. He looked threatening, but he was actually a gentle spirit who loved his aging grandmother enough to take time out of his busy ranch schedule to play Indian wars with her. She would have to watch out for him and not let Song Bird spoil too many of his high notes.

Moon Dance leaned over and whispered to him. "You can open your eyes now."

After White Eagle opened his eyes, he gave her a smirk grin and then winked. Then, he went to moaning and groaning like they had half killed him with the little prick. Moon Dance helped him to his feet. "I think you should go to your bedroom and lay down for awhile. Your fainting has left you with an eye twitch. It could be serious. I will make you a cup of stiff cactus tea and bring it to you. You may die before night from your wound and the twitching."

"You won't tell Night Hawk I fainted, will you sis?" White Eagle asked grinning and winking again at her. He had learned to fake faint when he was a kid to get out of any situation Song Bird or Night Hawk thought up that he didn't want to participate in. This time, he hadn't expected to have Sleeping Moon read him like a book and let him get by with it. She had never done that before in all their years of raids, wars, or blood oaths. He looked into her eyes deeply. That is when he knew something was wrong. The color in Sleeping Moon's eyes was all wrong. Sleeping Moon had soft chocolate brown eyes with a tint of green in them. Their father was a green eyed white man and their mother was Native American. Whoever was in his sister's body had dark, black brown eyes. There was not a hint of green in them.

"We are blood brothers. I won't tell you fainted if you don't tell what you see." Moon Dance replied winking back at him and grinning. She could tell that he was seeing her and not his sister.

"I should be so lucky with Song Bird. She is probably going to blab her mouth big time about my fainting and Charlie Elkhorn is going to kill me when he sees his white tea towel with blood stains on it." He stated continuing the conversation and trying to figure out her eye thing.

"You are safe with us, White Eagle." Moon Dance stated helping him up and down the hall of the ranch house to his bedroom. "From this day forward, Song Bird and I will put you in charge of our pony reins. We will do the drawing of any blood that is necessary. We won't make you watch. It is not pleasant to watch a grown warrior faint at the sight of blood."

"Blood . . ." he stated and pretended to half faint again. She grabbed his hand and held it.

"Sorry, I shouldn't have said that." Moon Dance replied quickly helping him into his room. Lie down on your bed and I will go for tea. Would you like a huge slice of lemon meringue pie to perk you up and make you feel better? I treat my captives well."

White Eagle lay down on his bed and patted the bed beside him. Moon Dance sat down on the side of the bed next to him. He took her hand and held it between his. After a moment or so of silence, he spoke. "Give me a few moments to recover and make a couple of necessary phone calls and then I will join you and Song Bird on a raid scaring the devil out of Night Hawk if you want. He has his woman friend out back of the barn in the camper. It is Saturday night."

"Making a camper raid is daring!" Moon Dance stated grinning.

"I think I am into a little camper shaking and running." He replied grinning and looking at her. He didn't let go of her hand. Then he asked. "You were a green tinted chocolate brown eyed Sleeping Moon when you entered the hospital for surgery. How and when did your eyes turn pure dark, black brown?"

Moon Dance didn't know what to say. How could she tell him that she was an Alien who had refused to board her space craft, killed her human body, and in spirit form took over his dead sister's body?

"I am a Kachina, a witch like the one across the river. I have learned to turn my eyes different colors with different hues of contact lens." She replied hoping he fell for the lie.

"That makes senses. When did you start wearing contacts?"

"Right after my surgery, the doctor recommended them."

"Did Charlie take you to town for them?"

"Charlie takes Song Bird and me everywhere. You are too busy with your lady friends at the Rio to worry about my eye doctor appointments." She laughed letting go of his hand "Meet Song Bird and I in the kitchen in ten minutes. I will tell her that we are going to do a little raiding and trailer shaking. It is a good day in the sight of the Great Spirit for such things. However, we women must take a powder room break first."

"That isn't a bad idea. The two of you tickled the pee-wad out of me. Let me have about five minutes and I will be right out." He stated winking at her again. She left his bedroom closing the door.

Lying on his bed, White Eagle gave his situation some thought. Should he be faithful to the Apache or turn traitor and return to the Arapaho? He considered all the pranks that Song Bird had pulled on him. She had cost him at least five lady friends in the last year. Traitor it was.

White Eagle sat up on the side of his bed and pulled his cell phone from his pocket to call Night Hawk and warn him so his three eyed Witch could exit the camper trailer before the Apache raid madness began. He knew that Night Hawk was in love with the Witch

In the meantime in the kitchen, Song Bird unlocked the glass china cabinet there and took down a prissy, pink flowered, china tea cup and held it to her ear. The previous year, she had a security company install a listening device in the cup and bugs in all the rooms of the house. She used it when necessary to listen to the private conversations of her grandchildren and cook. The rumor was that they were planning on trying to put her in a nursing home. She was one step ahead of them. She had made a new will disinheriting any grandchild that signed her commitment papers. She loved her grandchildren, but she would not be blindsided or stabbed in the back by them. The ranch was hers, not theirs. Plus, now she had an ally. Moon Dance was not Sleeping Moon. She had secretly hated the pampered, spoiled brat her real granddaughter was who often called her an old b . . . who should be put away. Moon Dance was respectful. She might just leave everything to her. Women always got the short end of the stick in life. She motioned for Moon Dance to come and listen to the teacup.

Moon Dance walked to the dish cabinet and took the flowered teacup from Song Bird and saw that there was a bugging listening device in it. She put it to her ear. White Eagle was saying something to Night Hawk and laughing about it. She handed it back to the grandmother.

"We have a low-life Arapaho spy in our camp, one that has sworn a blood oath to us. He makes plans with the Arapaho Chief Night Hawk to trick us into getting sprayed by a skunk out back at the travel trailer." Song Bird stated. She listened a few moments and then held the cup so that both of them could hear by putting the sides of their heads together with the cup between their ears.

They listened a moment or two as White Eagle first spoke on his cell phone to their cook, Charlie Elkhorn, telling about how he had been taken captive and where Charlie could find his dishwasher door. That was low. He was a snitch, an Arapaho snitch. Then they listened as White Eagle then rang Night Hawk's cell phone.

"When did you have this listening device installed in the tea cup?" Moon Dance asked in a whisper.

Song Bird giggled like a young school girl and then replied. "When Sleeping Moon was in the hospital, I had it secretly installed while my two grandsons were in the city sitting with her. Sleeping Moon was threatening to have me committed to a nursing home after she recovered. She wanted her share of the ranch so she could move away with her lesbian lover, Janice. I felt alone and like I needed an edge on them. They had run Tall Willow, my lover, off and put him in a nursing home. I was sure that I was next. That is why I have been slow in warming up you. I disinherited Sleeping Moon while she was in the hospital due to her disrespect of me. I have a new will. My ranch will be divided between all of my ranch hands and my grandsons. My grandsons will get a ranch hand's portion for their disrespect of me and Tall Willow."

"They are going to be as the white man says, pissed when your will is read. However, your ranch hands are going to be elated."

"I am fond of my lemon meringue pie eating ranch hands. I run a pie under their noses and they will do anything for me including turning Apache when needed. I also sign their pay checks."

"You are one smart Apache, Song Bird. I lift my braid and salute you with it. Don't you feel a little guilty leaving the larger portion of your ranch to strangers?"

"My ranch hands have been with me for years. They are family." She replied and then added. "White Eagle and Night Hawk get nothing if they contest my new will. They are old enough to get out and buy ranches of their own and run them. Of course, White Eagle is my heart. I might feel just a wee bit sad about his getting the shaft. However, my bugging device has now caught him turning traitor on me."

"So the bugging device is your way of staying captain of this ranch ship?"

"There is a bug in their rooms, the travel trailer, and the hay loft. If they sneak a lady friend in thru their window, I know it. I know just when to walk down the ranch house hallway, face their door and start singing opera. Raiding the enemy camp is my specialty. My other listening device is in a pink china cup in my bedroom on my knick knack shelf. They pay no attention to prissy pink flowered teacups."

"You are one smart Apache woman." Moon Dance laughed. I will remember this one when I am old. In my tribe of kachina Weelo Witches, we honor the aging of the tribe. A new chief, no matter what his age, will take the oldest widow as his first wife to make sure she is honored and taken care of in her special years of wisdom. It is our way on Earth of caring for the elderly."

"Well, no one honors me around here, so I am married to this listening device. A girl has to do what a girl has to do." Song Bird stated putting the cup listening device back to her ear.

Moon dance laughed with her. At the same time, her own words saddened her. Had Gray Feather taken Hissing Cat because she was the oldest member of the New Mexico Weelo tribe? The rule had been made to protect and provide for the elderly women of the tribe?

"Don't be an old fool!" Moon Dance muttered dismissing the thought. Pansy Skywalker was not an aging member of the tribe. Gray Feather slept with her and gave her a child which was a marriage. It was a harsh reality to face. She was indeed an old fool and the never ending nightmare was going to haunt her soul forever.

CHAPTER FOURTEEN

A SKUNK OF A TRAITOR

Having finished his conversation with Charlie Elkhorn, White Eagle rang Night Hawk's cell phone and waited for him to answer. He was a captive Indian who was now planning his escape and the taking of the Apache tribe's ponies. It was a good day to be at war with the women. He didn't have anything better to do. It was Saturday and he was currently without a steady girlfriend. He didn't attract lots of women like Night Hawk did. Sometimes he lied about having a woman at the Rio Inn or in his bedroom. His thick glasses were not appealing to some women and he couldn't see without them.

"What is up?" Night Hawk asked answering in an annoyed voice. "This better be good, White Eagle. I am busy at the moment, if you know what I mean."

"Get your witch out of the camper trailer. Song Bird and Sleeping Moon are headed your way in five to ten minutes. Do we still have that wild boar caged down behind the barn, the one we planned to take to the processing plant?"

"Yes . . . why?"

"I have been captured by the Apache but plan to use my captivity to our advantage. Grab one of the ranch hands and close the boar up in the camper. I will escort my two female captors back there letting them think we are in for a little trailer shaking and high notes. Leave the door loose. The caged wild boar will be mad, jump out, scare them, and hopefully chase them. Don't we have a little getting even to do for a few of Song Bird's high notes? By the way, who is with you? That voice doesn't sound like that of your Rio Witch."

"Millie is here from the diner. The Rio Witch dumped me, in case you haven't heard. Song Bird caused it. My Witch is afraid of song Bird. She told me to take a hike because she didn't want to deal with Song Bird's madness. I am definitely game for a little revenge." Night Hawk stated sitting up in the camper trailer bed ignoring Millie who was half drunk.

White Eagle laughed and then lowered his voice. "I thought you and the witch were serious about each other?"

"We will discuss that another time. I will get Millie up and out of here. Have one of the ranch hands grab his rifle in case the boar gets a little too close to them. I don't want them hurt, just the hell scared out of them." Night Hawk replied handing Millie her jeans and t-shirt.

"Song Bird has scared the Hell out of my last five girl friends. I am tired of getting dumped because of her opera high notes." White Eagle replied knowing he was lying. He didn't currently have a girl friend. He spent his Saturday nights alone at the Rio to keep face.

"On second thought, I've got a better idea than the boar. Charlie has a live skunk trapped and caged. He plans to turn it loose at the upcoming barbecue over at the Masons. In case you have forgotten, John Mason put vodka in the punch bowl last year at his sister's wedding and the women were too drunk for us to dance with or hit any high notes with."

"Yea, I remember. That was one sloppy drunk wedding reception. I don't think the bride ever cut her cake. You have to give Mason credit. His sister's daughters were all safe from us for the evening."

Night Hawk laughed. "Even Millie here was drunk as a skunk and she can usually hold her liquor pretty well. She has sworn off wedding punch."

"Are you sure you want to waste a good skunk on our two crazy women?" White Eagle asked. "A skunk isn't the easiest creature to trap and cage."

"I will help Charlie come up with a new plan for the Mason's barbecue. Our women are definitely getting sprayed with a perfume they aren't spending our money for." Night Hawk laughed. "As I recall, they spiked our after shave bottles last week with garlic juice. I think it just might be worth taking a tomato juice bath, to cause them to stink worse than we did last week."

"I am willing to do the tomato juice bath bit myself, just to get them sprayed." White Eagle replied snorting.

"The Arapaho tribe is on the war path!" Night Hawk stated laughing and then shook his woman for the evening. "Get up Millie and get out of here. Song Bird is on the way."

"I will stall Moon Dance and Song Bird for fifteen minutes. Then I will head that way with them. By the way, Sleeping Moon is now Moon Dance. Grandmother Song Bird has decided to rename her."

"Moon Dance, huh?"

"Have you noticed that Sleeping Moon is different since she had her surgery? I can't put my finger on it. You know that she and I were always at odds with each other. Our new Moon Dance or Sleeping Moon held my hand tonight and I felt like we bonded. I like the new person she is!"

"The Rattlesnake hunter in her I can do without." Night Hawk retorted. "You do know that she drew a snake in the bottom of Charlie Elkhorn's cigar box warning him to back off. He told me about it earlier when I was talking with him."

"Our sister has a whole new personality, Night Hawk. That is what I am talking about. She is a strong force and holds her own with us. I like the Rattlesnake hunter in her. If she weren't my sister, I might be interested in her. She could keep me in line. Our old Sleeping moon was a spoiled brat who talked about nothing but nail polish colors, the latest fashions, and her soap opera with the heart doctor in it. Our new sister has never mentioned her old frivolous interests or the medical TV series."

"I will pay a little closer attention and tell you want I think. Maybe the lack of oxygen when she died left her a little slow and she just doesn't remember the things she used to be interested in."

"You are probably right. Even if she is a little slower in her thinking, I like the new sister we have." White Eagle replied.

"The boys and I will place the skunk in a cage underneath the camper trailer door. Make sure she opens the door to aggravate the skunk. The boys and I will hide out behind the bunk house and be more than happy to give our women a good round of male laughter when they get sprayed."

"I hear someone. Fifteen Minutes." White Eagle stated flipping his cell phone closed and quickly laying back down on his bed.

The sound in the hallway was actually Charlie Elkhorn who, after parking his jeep in the front drive, entered by the front door. The front door was never used except for company. Today was different. On his way to town, a flock of Ravens had flown down and landed in the middle of the black top in front of him. They prevented him from going on without running over them. They wouldn't fly off even when he got out of his jeep and tried to scare them. He took it as a sign to return to the ranch house. He was Indian. He believed in signs. A black raven was not a good sign.

Arriving back at the ranch house, a coyote was sitting blocking the driveway that wound around to the back of the house and the kitchen. He was forced to use the front entrance. This spooked him big time and he feared that something might have happened to Sleeping Moon and that was the reason the Great Spirit's creatures blocked his path. He was Indian first and Catholic second. He was both superstitious and religious.

As he was making his way down the long hallway to the kitchen he heard White Eagle's voice planning to skunk spray the two women of the house. He wasn't sure how he felt about that. He was part of the men's tribe of Arapaho in their play and prank raids, but Sleeping Moon was just a couple of months or so out of the hospital. He wasn't sure that skunk scent and tomato juice baths were a wise thing to submit her to, especially since she had been asthmatic her whole life. He was concerned and took it from the signs given him that he was to cross over to the Apache tribe for the night. The Ravens had to mean that Sleeping Moon could possibly die from the spraying. The coyote had pointed him in a direction to over hear White Eagle's conversation. He had recently developed feelings for Sleeping Moon, even though she didn't seem to see him as a man. He respected a woman who could capture Rattlesnakes with her bare hands. He needed a woman who could capture and own his wild side.

Charlie Elkhorn made his way back to the kitchen not sure of what to do about the situation. He walked in on two surprised women who quickly put away a prissy, pink, flowered china cup in the top of the china cabinet. Song Bird then quickly locked the dish cabinet's glass door.

"May I ask what you two Apache women are doing in my kitchen?" He asked not seeing yet that his dishwasher had its door missing.

"We just had tea." Grandmother Song Bird replied and quickly started heading for the back door of the kitchen to exit.

"Yes, we just had tea." Moon Dance added quickly following on Song Bird's heels. She and Song Bird were toast if he spotted the missing dishwasher door before they managed to exit.

"Why are you in such a hurry?"He called. Stay and have a cup of coffee with me!"

"The hum . . . sputtered Song Bird backing out the back door. "I hear it and I must go check on it."

"Yes, the hum . . . we are going to see where it is coming from. It sounds like a coyote with a bad singing voice."Moon Dance stated searching for something to say as she backed out the door.

"This is not a good sign . . . "he muttered watching them close the door. "They are up to something." He then walked over to the back door and looked out its window pane. He watched Song Bird and Moon Dance running for the barn.

Charlie Elkhorn turned back to the kitchen and that is when he saw his dishwasher door was missing. He belted out a wild, mad, Indian war cry of a scream that could be heard clear to the barn. He had been a victim of an Apache raid and the Great Spirit had tried to warn him. If he hadn't stopped to check the mail on the way in, he would have caught them. He pulled off his western hat and threw it violently on the floor. Then he made the sign of the cross. The Great Spirit or his Catholic God had tried to warn him. He didn't know which. He would thank both.

White Eagle left his bedroom and flew to the kitchen hearing Charlie Elkhorn's war cry of a scream.

"What is wrong?" White Eagle shouted entering the kitchen with his pistol drawn. Everyone at the ranch carried pistols in case a border crosser might try to break in. Seeing Charlie Elkhorn staring at his dishwasher, he lowered his pistol and put it away.

"They got you!" White Eagle laughed as he watched Charlie examine the missing door and then a blood stained tea towel in his sink.

"They have stolen my door and killed an animal. I don't know where they have hidden the critter. It will probably rot and smell in here before I figure out where. I shouldn't have fried the legs of that frog. Sleeping Moon is out to get me now."

White Eagle immediately stuck his hand behind his back. He was the wild animal that the two women had cut.

"We are getting even in about twenty minutes, Charlie. A rotting animal in your kitchen will be minor compared to how they will soon smell. "Come along with me. We have an Arapaho revenge raid on our women using your trapped skunk as our weapon of choice. It is going to be sweet; or should I say smelly?"

Charlie Elkhorn considered the prank that Night Hawk and White Eagle planned to pull off. In spite of being angry over the dishwasher door, he could not be part of a prank that might be detrimental to Sleeping Moon's health. He knew that she was asthmatic and the skunk scent might just set her off in a violent, life threatening attack. He didn't understand why her two brothers felt she was okay now that she had a fixed heart. Asthma was a whole different ailment.

"Go do your thing White Eagle. I must repair this door, get the blood out of my tea towel, and figure out where the rotting animal is. I will plan my own revenge. You and I will have to admit that their taking my dishwasher door off was pretty ingenious." He stated starting to get over being mad.

"I want you to pull all the cans of tomato juice from the pantry. We are going to need them for the women to bathe in after we get them sprayed." White Eagle laughed walking out the back door.

Charlie Elk Horn pretended to be busy till he left. Then, he stepped to the back door to see where he was heading. The women had headed to hide in the barn. He saw that White Eagle was headed for the camper that sat in a field behind the barn out near the bunkhouse. Even though he was mad about the dishwasher door, he would warn Sleeping Moon and Song Bird. A prank was one thing, but putting someone at risk was another thing. He would turn traitor for the rest of the evening and join the women's Apache tribe.

When White Eagle was out of sight, Charlie Elkhorn opened the back door and headed for the barn. Knowing Songbird, he figured the front door would be rigged with some sort of trap. He walked around to the side of the barn and climbed thru one of the windows of the horse's stalls. He patted a Palomino gently on its neck after climbing in to keep the horse quiet. Then he let himself out of the stall. He saw Sleeping Moon and Song bird hiding just inside the barn door. He scanned the barn door. Song Bird had rigged the door with a bucket of water above it. He grinned. She probably had it rigged for him. He would slip back out and see that it was one of the two brothers who got the treatment. He exited quietly thru the Palomino's stall and back out the window and headed for the travel trailer. Night Hawk and the ranch hands had a caged skunk on the end of a long pole. With bandanas over their noses, they were carrying the caged skunk preparing to stick it just under the travel trailer door.

The plan was for the women to step up to the travel trailer door; and then get sprayed by the mad skunk. The ranch hands had quickly teased the bunk house dogs with raw steaks and then dropped the meat down into the Skunk's cage. From their hiding place on the end of the bunkhouse, they planned to turn the dogs loose to aggravate the skunk when the women stepped up to the travel trailer's door making sure they got sprayed.

"What is up?" Charlie Elkhorn asked Night Hawk.

"I hear the Apache tribe of women managed to raid your kitchen camp." Night Hawk stated with a smirk as he motioned the ranch hands to hide behind the far end of the bunkhouse.

"I am still looking for the door, they hid it. Just so you know, Sleeping Moon and Song Bird are hiding just inside the front door of the barn. They are hiding from me. I used a few choice words when I found the dishwasher door missing. I think you might have to entice them to leave their hiding spot."

"Since when do you use foul language, Elkhorn?"

"Since I came to work for you and I have had to put up with your sister and Song Bird. They both know how to bring the worst out of a man."

"They are forces to deal with." Night Hawk replied. "I have to give you credit. You have stayed the longest of any housekeeper cook we have ever had. Most of them stay six weeks tops."

"I like crazy women. Bimbo bleached blondes don't do it for me. I like crazy."

"Thank God. I don't know what I would do without you. I am sorry that you have been saddled with the extra work of caring for Sleeping Moon. I have another ad running. I am trying to find a nurse companion for her."

"Your new sister is growing on me and I don't mind the extra work."

"White Eagle said the same thing. He said she was a new person. I am going to have to take some time to see what the two of you are talking about. Where did you say Song Bird and my sister are hiding?"

"They are just inside the barn door peeping out. I think you should slip in the front door at just the right moment when I hum pretending to be an alien. You know how fearful Song Bird is of aliens. When I hum, you step in the barn door to supposedly protect them. State you heard humming. I will slip in the barn thru one of the horse stall windows and hum behind them. When I start humming, you enter the front and then tell them to go stay in the travel trailer and keep your witch safe till you check the barn and the humming out. Song Bird will be more than happy to go meet your witch. Sleeping Moon will just follow Song Bird's lead. They will get sprayed when they knock on the camper trailer door." Charlie Elkhorn stated laughing.

"That is a pretty good plan, Elkhorn. It is just simple enough to work."

"Just give me time to get thru the horse stall window before you enter the front door. I have to have time to hum and frighten them. This will be one to tell your witch and friends about at the next campfire."

"My lady friend down by the Rio is not a witch, Charlie. She just has a bad scar. She had a huge mole removed from her forehead, a birth defect, and it left an indented recess that is eye shaped. The jewel she wears in it makes it look like it is an eye. She is unique, Charlie, and has made the most of her imperfection. People are cruel calling her a witch. However, she has taken people's cruelty and her uniqueness and created a life for herself. She has taught herself to read the Tarot and she scares a few people rattling some chicken bones."Night hawk replied.

"Song Bird thinks your witch is a humming Kachina." Charlie Elkhorn replied. "She thinks that she might be an alien."

"It doesn't matter. My Witch broke up with me. She is afraid of Song Bird and told me she doesn't want to deal with Song Bird's madness."

"I don't blame her. Song Bird gets the best of me sometimes." Charlie replied laughing.

"It is time to get this skunk raid on the way." White Eagle stated walking up to Night Hawk and Charlie Elkhorn. The caged skunk was in place beneath the travel trailer door and White Eagle was now about to escort the ranch hands around the corner of the bunk house to hide and watch.

"One of the two of you will have to entice the women from the barn." White Eagle stated. They think I am on their side, it can't be me. Plus, I smell. They might guess that we are up to something."

"Night Hawk is going to entice them out after I sneak in the back of the barn and start humming. That should scare them right into Night Hawks arms. He will send them to the travel trailer to meet his lady friend and keep her safe." Elkhorn stated knowing he planned to take Sleeping Moon out the back of the barn thru a horse stall window to protect her from the skunk spray.

"We are ready." White Eagle stated and walked away motioning for the ranch hands to hide around the far corner of the bunkhouse out of sight.

Night Hawk and Charlie Elkhorn stood watching the ranch hands disappear. There were eight of them. The Seven Moons Ranch was huge.

"Just so you know, Charlie, I would marry my witch who lives down by the Rio if she would have me. She keeps turning me down because of Song Bird. Now, she has broken up with me. Millie is my back burner, good -times girl. However, I am not going to see Millie any more after tonight. I plan to suck up my injured pride and go see my Rio Witch and ask her what I can do to settle the Song Bird problem between us. I love her and want to marry her."

"Marry Song Bird off to Tall Willow, the old dude from Mason's ranch that went in to the nursing home last year. They could live together in the nursing home and share a room. Your witch could take over the position as head of the ranch house."

"That isn't possible, Charlie. I don't own the ranch. Song Bird owns it and whoever she chooses to hand it down to. I am not exactly her favorite grandchild. White Eagle is! She prefers him even to Sleeping Moon. If Song Bird marries the old humming dude and he out lives her, he inherits."

"So that is why you and White Eagle got rid of the old guy."

"I admit, I am a little guilty of greed as well as protecting my sibling's backsides. Sleeping Moon would be devastated if this ranch was jerked out from under her. It is her home. She isn't healthy enough to work and make a living. The ranch supports all of us well. I can't see myself as a ranch hand working for someone else. This ranch is my life."

"So getting rid of the old guy was an insurance policy."

"A man has to do what a man has to do. White Eagle and I have poured our hearts and souls into this ranch. We haven't married nor had kids. I am twenty nine years old and don't have my first child yet. Song Bird isn't thinking straight.

Who knows how many kids the old dude has that would inherit what belongs to us."

"Did you hear the humming earlier?" Charlie asked looking around. "I heard it earlier outside the farmhouse. Could it be the old guy humming and letting Song Bird know that he is back?"

"I will hum his ass if I catch him. You would think that a thirty mile ride in the night air with no clothes on in the back of a poop filled horse trailer would have cured his courting ass. Maybe more drastic measures are needed. You would think, at the age of ninety-one, you would lose your desire to hum."

"If I live to be ninety, I hope I remember how to hum." Charlie Elkhorn retorted grinning and then continued, "And with your sister."

"What?"

"You heard me. I have been meaning to talk to you about it. I want permission to call on and marry Sleeping Moon. I think she is the one for me!" Charlie Elkhorn replied.

Night Hawk laughed and headed for the barn half yelling over his shoulder. "Good luck! She will have you sleeping with a Rattlesnake, if you cross her. Court her if you have the nerve. She is one wild, crazy Indian and a lesbian."

"I need a wild, crazy Indian woman to tame my ways!" Charlie yelled back ignoring the lesbian comment. "She won't take any crap off of me. Plus, she is Catholic like me."

CHAPTER FIFTEEN

SURPRISE IN THE BARN

Charlie Elkhorn made his way around the barn and once more crawled quietly thru the horse stall window. He patted the Palomino again to keep him quiet. Then he quietly exited the stall and crept till he was standing behind Sleeping Moon. He then quickly put his hand over her mouth and dragged her back into one of the horse stalls whispering to her to be quiet that he was saving her from Nigh Hawk.

Sleeping Moon squirmed and fought, but she was no match for Charlie Elkhorn. Crouching with her secured in one arm and his other hand over her mouth, they watched thru the rails of the horse stall. She tried to make a sound. It came out like a high pitched hum out of her nose. She decided that wasn't such a good idea because it might frighten Song Bird who was afraid of hummers.

"Be quiet . . . ! Night Hawk and the ranch hands plan to lure you out to the camper and into a trap with a skunk. I am saving your dishwasher door, stealing ass." He stated holding her securely.

Moon Dace could feel Charlie Elkhorn's heart beating as she was held with her back tightly to him. She had forgotten what it was like to feel a man's heart beat. She wasn't sure that she wanted him to let her go. Charlie ignored her as he hummed and eyed the bucket of water over the barn door. He kept his hand over Sleeping Moon's mouth so she couldn't warn Song Bird.

Charlie Elkhorn was finding pleasure in humming and frightening Song Bird. The grandmother had put a tarantula one morning last week in his coffee pot. When he went to make coffee, the spider had jumped out at him scaring the pee wad out of him. It was payback time. He hummed and could see her squirming. She was afraid of humming. He was sure that she would half kill him and threaten to fire him when the prank of the men's was over. However, he wasn't going anywhere. Night Hawk couldn't find house help to deal with her and Sleeping Moon.

Moon Dance quit struggling realizing that there was no use. Charlie was a tall, muscular, Indian man. She was no match for him. She would just have to let the barn episode play itself out. She definitely didn't have Song Bird's back door and White Eagle was a traitor.

Then the door opened and Night Hawk stepped quickly inside hearing the humming. Immediately, Song Bird released the rope on the bucket and five gallons of bleach water fell with a splash drenching the unsuspecting Night Hawk who had on his good western hat and boots. He was soaked from head to foot and was sputtering and spitting and gagging from the bleach stench.

"I am going to kill the two of you." He yelled when he managed to catch his breath and get the mess wiped from his face with the back of his hand. He took off his new black felt western hat and threw it on the ground with force saying a few choice words. It was turning a funny shade of spotted gray from the bleach.

"You are the hummer?" Song Bird asked looking surprised. Charlie had quit humming in the back of the barn and was forcing Moon Dance to climb thru the back window of the stall.

Night Hawk went to laughing in spite of being mad. "I give up. You win this Indian raid. Would you like to come out to the trailer and meet my lady friend, the Witch? I am not going to be able to explain how I look and smell to her. You might as well have the pleasure. You can visit with her while I go up to the main house and change."

"It is not safe to leave your lady friend by herself. The hummers are here tonight." Song Bird stated with big eyes. They were humming just before you entered. They might steal your witch from you and she would never be seen again, like your mother."

"I doubt if any hummer is going to mess with my witch. She can hold her own. She casts spells with chicken bones and looks into the other world with her big, ruby jewel third eye." Night Hawk stated trying to amuse his grandmother and coax her out to the camper trailer to get sprayed. He didn't see Sleeping Moon. He would have to get her later. She had to be hiding.

"About that time, Charlie Elkhorn broke thru the front door of the barn. "Hurry, Night Hawk! Sleeping Moon made a run for the safety of the travel trailer. The skunk sprayed her and set her asthma off. I have called for the paramedics. She doesn't look good. We laid her down in the camper and White Eagle is giving her mouth to mouth. She is dying I think."

"Oh shit . . . "Night Hawk stated with all of the blood draining from his face believing Charlie Elkhorn and forgetting about the prank. He ran from the barn and toward the trailer that now had its lights on inside. He flew to the door forgetting the skunk. When he opened it, the skunk sprayed him good. He ignored the skunk and went ahead and opened the door thinking that Sleeping Moon was half dead. The camper trailer was empty. That is when he knew he had been had. Charlie Elkhorn, for some reason, had crossed over to the Apache tribe. He turned around to see all of the ranch hands pouring out from the end of the bunk house.

"We got you!" The ranch hands yelled loudly thinking that it was Song Bird or Sleeping Moon that had been sprayed. They quickly became quiet seeing their boss soaking wet as well as smelling like a skunk. They quickly got lost snorting and laughing as they went.

"C h a r l i e . . . E l k . . . h o r n! I am going to kill you when I catch up with you!" Night Hawk yelled loudly at the top of his lungs. Then there was the sound of him choking, gagging, and spitting.

A tomato juice shower was taken, but it wasn't Moon Dance or Song Bird who took it. Fate had smiled on them and Charlie Elkhorn had joined the Apache tribe, at least for the present.

Outside the barn, Charlie Elkhorn made his way back to Moon Dance who he had left leaning against the side of the barn in the shadows of a monstrous Weeping Willow. She grinned at him and hugged him when he reached her. She had listened and heard it all. Charlie Elkhorn had saved her and Song Bird from getting sprayed.

"Why did you choose to help me and Song Bird? I stole your door and your cigars."

"Your safety is more important to me that your brothers playing a prank on you. The skunk scent could have caused you some serious problems with your asthma." He stated wrapping his arms around her. It was a moment that he had fantasized about. She actually had her arms around him.

"I heard you humming." She added not letting go but leaning her face against his chest. "Are you the one who hums to frighten everyone around here?"

"I am not Song Bird's hummer, but I am now yours because you have heard me." He laughed. "It is our secret. Occasionally, I hum to annoy Song Bird and the boys."

"I can feel your heart beat on my face. For some reason, I have never seen you as a man with a heartbeat. I like the rhythm of it. I don't have a heart beat anymore."

"What do you mean you don't have a heart beat?" he asked eyeing her.

He wanted to tell her how much he was in love with her. The strange thing was, he didn't love her before her surgery. She was different back then, a spoiled brat that was petted and pampered because she was ill. Since she had come home from the hospital, there was something about her eyes. Not only that, he liked the fact that she wasn't scared of Rattlesnakes or anything. Before surgery, she wouldn't have lifted a manicured finger to take off a dishwasher door, and would have run at the sight of a snake screeching like a wild kachina. He liked who she was now. However, it was her eyes that he was in love with. He couldn't put his finger on what he saw in them. However, he knew she was way more than human. She was divine and he wanted her.

"I floated thru the dream catcher in my room and gave its hands the many pieces of my heart."

"What do you mean you floated thru the dream catcher? They are created to catch nightmares. I gave you the one in your room for a birthday gift a few years ago." He replied in a confused voice.

"I was a spirit in the between worlds with a shattered heart and I entered Sleeping Moon's body when she died on the operating table. She gave me her abandoned body to live in. A man shattered my heart in another life time. In my bedroom, I floated thru the dream catcher and gave it my broken heart willingly. Now I do not have one. Afterward, I floated back into this body and now dwell without a heart. I am not Sleeping Moon, Charlie Elkhorn. I am a witch like Night Hawks woman down by the Rio."

"Are you telling me that you are a mythical, heartless kachina, a stealer of human souls and bodies?" he asked.

Moon Dance took his hand and placed it across her heart area. There was no beat. Charlie Elkhorn quickly released her and stepped back a couple of steps in fright.

"I am like Night Hawk's witch. I am a Kachina who walks between worlds. Tonight, I felt your heart beat and I want to be loved by it. I am really lonely."

"Are you going to steal my heart beat or my soul?" he asked eyeing her and standing back. He was Indian and he was frightened. His mother had raised him with frightening stories of Kachina who came and snatched children and men's souls and bodies.

"Sleeping Moon's body, that I am in, is dying. When it takes its last breath, I must find a new body to enter and live in till I return to the home of my soul."

Tears came to Charlie's eyes. He was in love with her and her words of dying bothered him. However, her words of being a Kachina frightened the hell out of him.

"I love you Sleeping Moon. You have to be spoofing or pulling a prank on me!

I asked Night Hawk tonight for permission to date you."

"I am not Sleeping Moon, Charlie. I am Moon Dance, a three eyed Kachina. I live in Sleeping Moon's body. She gave it to me when she died in the hospital and she, as a soul, discarded it. I am Moon Dance, a catcher of Rattlesnakes, a witch, and a Kachina medicine woman."

"Is that what I see in your eyes?"

"Yes. I am a stranger in this body. I am not Sleeping Moon. She has crossed over."

"I hated the Sleeping Moon that existed before surgery. You, I am in love with." He stated rolling over her new name in his mouth. "Moon . . . Dance . . .!"

"Your arms felt wonderful around me, Charlie Elkhorn. Is that why you put the plastic green frog in my oatmeal? Were you attracted to me and trying to get my attention?"

"I am not exactly God's gift to women. I am a ranch house cook. The answer to your frog question is yes. I am in love with you and would like to marry you. I want you."

"Would you be willing to sleep in my bed, even if I am a kachina? Suppose I am a spirit who must step from body to body to survive and live in several women's bodies while loving you?"

"Are you telling me that you are a dark demon who can possess humans? Are you asking me to make a league with the devil?"

"No, I am asking if you can love me if I am different from ordinary human women. You, as an Indian, call the different ones witches and Kachina. I am one of them."

"Don't joke with me Moon Dance. We, on this ranch, are Catholic. We do not form alliances with darkness or demons. That would damn our souls. However, Night Hawk is about to damn his. He plans to ask the three eyed witch down by the Rio to marry him."

"I am tired of being alone, Charlie Elkhorn. I am willing to take you for a permanent mate and take you wherever I go. I have the ability."

Moon Dance then stepped away from him a few feet. With one finger, she ran a line down from the top of her head to her heart area and let Sleeping Moon's head and shoulders slip from her revealing her blue, three eyed Weelo self with black hair, crystal ears, and three eyes.

Charlie Elkhorn began to tremble in shock. "Holy Mother of God . . ." He stated making the sign of the cross. "Get the behind me Satan. I am Catholic. I will not join forces with darkness. Whoever you are, you have cast a spell on my heart, but I will not give into your seduction of me. You are a demon! Get thee behind me just as Christ told the devil on the night of his temptation. I am a good Catholic."

Charlie Elkhorn then turned his back on Moon Dance and sprinted away in fright. Moon Dance burst into tears. She was far from being a force of darkness. She was just a woman from another planet needing a friend, a companion, and someone to grow old in human years with. She was devastated that he thought she was a dark force, one of the Earth's fictitious demons. She knew she was a good person and had given her best to all who had asked anything of her, including Gray Feather. Moon Dance was sorry that Charlie rejected her. She could have been happy sleeping in his bed and having him to cling to in the night. She didn't have a heart to love, but she was sure that she could have made him happy.

One more man had declared his love for her and then abandoned her. She wondered what was so hideous about herself that made men walk away from her. She wanted to be held, adored, and loved. Also, she wanted to love and adore a man. Sleeping Moon's human body may have been a lesbian, she was not.

CHAPTER SIXTEEN

TALL WILLOW RETURNS

Leaning against the ranch house in the dark, Moon Dance wiped tears from her eyes. Another rejection was a hard pill to swallow. She would love to have curled up in Charlie Elkhorn's arms for the night. She was so lonely. Wiping her eyes, she turned her attention to the sudden sound of someone humming. She started to scan the ranch grounds to see where it was coming from.

Looking down the winding drive, she spotted a tall figure walking toward the ranch house. It was a male wearing all white western attire including a white hat. He was humming a tune that she was not familiar with. She watched as the tall figure turned off the main drive and started walking down a side dirt road toward the barn.

That is when Moon dance realized that Song Bird could possibly still be in the barn hiding after the skunk event. She was alarmed because she didn't recognize the stranger. Forgetting her own misery and rejection, she started walking in the shadows following the man in white western wear. When it was very obvious that he was headed for the barn and not the bunkhouse, she panicked and started speeding up her walk to a quiet sprint till she reached him. She grabbed him by the arm turning him around and drew the pistol from her long, teal colored, cotton skirt and pointed it at him.

"Who are you and what are you doing here?" Moon Dance asked trying not to appear afraid.

"I am Tall Willow, Song Bird's friend. Who are you?" He asked arching one of his white bushy eyebrows.

"I am a kachina, a Seven Moons Ranch Witch. You are not supposed to be here. If night Hawk catches you, it is a horse trailer ride for you."

The tall elderly man grinned. His hair was snow white and he had bushy eyebrows that needed a woman to clip them out of his eyes. Even his eyelashes had turned white, or were they a light shade of purple?

"You are not a Kachina or a witch. I can tell by your eyes. You are like me, an alien. I am from Planet Plutonia. Where are you from?"

"I am Weelo. What are you doing here and why are you humming? Everyone here knows that Grandmother Song Bird is frightened to death of humming."

"She is not afraid of my sound. I hum to let her know I am here. However, she does not know that I am Plutonian. I have worked this incarnation as a ranch hand on the Mason spread next door. Tonight, I go home to Plutonia. I have come for Song Bird to take her with me. A light port is being sent for the two of us and it will arrive in an hour."

"Oh . . . Night Hawk and White Eagle will be devastated." She replied in shock and then added. "They will think some border crosser has kidnapped her and possibly left her body in the desert somewhere. They will not understand having no body to bury."

"It will be Song Bird's decision, if I can convince her to go. I will travel in Spirit form, but she must go in her human form. I do not have the ability to unzip a live human. I don't know how she will take it when I unzip this body and she sees a man with purple skin and three eyes."

"I understand more than you will ever know, Tall Willow. A man declared his love for me about half an hour ago and walked away when I tried to explain and show him who I am. He insinuated I had to be a dark force, a devil. Why do humans brand anyone different from them as devils?"

"That is a good question, Moon Dance. I am not looking forward to showing Song Bird that I am not Tall Willow."

"If Song Bird should refuse to go with you, may I take the light port home with you? I could catch a space craft from there and fly home to Weelo. I have had my fill of humans and what they call love. I am thinking of buying a place in the mountains on Planet Jupella, the fourth moon of Weelo. "

"Why in the hell would you want to do that? It is uncivilized. I think there might be fifty people total scattered and living around its surface." You would be living an eternity of hermit existence."

"Right now, Tall Willow, it sounds pretty good."

"But won't you be lonely?"

"Loneliness is preferable to running into your nightmare on a regular basis. A human I fell in love with, by the name of Gray Feather, broke my heart and chose to marry two women ahead of me. I have given my shattered heart to the dream catcher's hands. I am dead on the inside and will never love again."

"I see in your eyes that you have had a really bad experience loving a human?"

"Human love hurts. I never want to experience it again. If you will take me home with you in the port, I will become a hermit on Planet Jupella where I will not bump into him. My hair dresser took him home with her on the Great Mother Ship. She married him just before it arrived."

"I sincerely wish I could offer you a ride home, but Plutonian light ports can only transport two. Fifty Earth years ago, the ports could only transport one. A lot of Plutonians were forced to leave behind human mates they really loved when returning by port home."

"I understand and wish you and Song Bird the best. She has told me about you. I will turn my back when you take her and not tell anyone. I respect how the two of you feel about each other. My Earth love, Gray Feather, took my hair dresser home with him. My heart shattered when I discovered they were married. The only way I could deal with it was to stay here and give the pieces of my broken heart to the nightmare hands of the dream catcher. I am now a cold woman, but still want to go home to Weelo."

"Ouch, as the humans say." He replied looking intently into her eyes as though he were reading her.

"May I share your port if Song Bird turns you down?" Moon Dance asked as she once more looked him over. He was very attractive for an old man. His tall, thin human body was definitely Native American. White western wear suited him. He looked a bit like an angel all dressed in white. He looked like a God with his white hair, white eyebrows, and white mustache. Song Bird was one lucky woman.

"I will take you, should Song Bird turn me down. However, I am certain she loves me and will go with me. I am dreading unzipping and showing her who I really am. She is used to this tall western looking Indian man. I am afraid she is going to see me and my purple skin as a shock. However, we love each other. I am sure she will accept me for who I am."

"If I don't leave with you by port, I am walking away from this ranch tonight when everyone sleeps. I plan to discard this body and choose another. I am not happy in my existence here on the ranch and I cannot face Charlie Elkhorn the cook at breakfast in the morning. He insulted me and called me a female demon. I will float along the shore of the winding Rattlesnake Rio and find a new human body to dwell in. I may join the witch down by the Rio, read the Tarot, and rattle a few chicken bones."

Tall Willow reached over in compassion and took Moon Dance in his elderly arms and held her close. "I am sorry you have had no one to truly love you. Song Bird and I have been lucky to have each other."

Moon Dance nuzzled her ear against his heart area. The beat of his heart was a pleasant one. She had so wanted to be held by a man with a respectful heart beat. "You have a singing heart beat, Tall Willow. Song Bird is lucky to be able to lean in your arms and listen to its magic song of love."

Tall Willow continued holding her sensing that she needed his arms. "I listened to Astral Planetary News the other night while servicing the light port opening here. There was a newscast report about the Great Mother Ship Noah II and its rescue of a lost tribe of Weelo from Planet Earth. The news report spoke of a great woman named Moon Dance who held the tribe together for thousands of years thru many incarnations who stayed on Earth on a search and rescue mission for those not making it in time to board."

"So that is the lie my tribe is telling to save face. They all disrespected me and should have been denied passage home. I did lead and keep my tribe together, but I stayed behind refusing to board with them and their disrespect. If I had gone home with them, they would all be in Weelo prisons for disrespecting me the captain of the space flyer. I gave them a gift of freedom. They don't realize it." She stated sadly and then asked. "Why do you dress in white? Plutonians usually choose purple."

"A man on Earth dressing in purple is considered a He/she. I have chosen to dress in white. It reminds me of the white mountains of home. My fellow ranch hands over at the Mason Ranch call me Whitey! Only Song bird calls me Tall Willow."

"What is your plutonian name?"

"Doctor Damn. I am a research scientist on mission here to study the desert . I have sent documents, drawings, and research specimen home by light port for the last seventy years. My time of service here is over. The light port comes for me tonight."

"You are the hummer in Song Bird's barn?"

"I am her hummer, but the hum she is frightened of is the hum the light port makes when it arrives and leaves again. Unfortunately, she and her husband built their barn over the light port heli-pad. My light port now opens its doors on the third floor of Song Bird's hay loft. Climbing that straight up ladder is getting to be a problem for this ninety year old human body. I am glad to be going home tonight. I had a hell of a time climbing out the second floor window of the human nursing home to make my way here."

"Well, Damn Tall Willow. I bet that name has got you a few snickers."

Tall Willow grinned. "Even my Song Bird ribs me. She yells when she sees me, 'There is my damn Tall Willow.'"

"It is a good thing Song Bird found you first. I would be claiming you for my damn Tall Willow. I am a scientist like you. I was aboard the Weelo Great Mother Ship when it crashed. We were harvesting Earth plants and animals for study. I am also a flight engineer. I have a thing for space flyers." Moon Dance replied and then added. "Did you know Sleeping Moon? She was Plutonian."

"I knew her. She kept Song Bird and her Earth brothers busy on the nights I needed to send items by port home to Plutonia. She would fake heart pains and keep them all at her bedside. She was my assistant. I knew our tour of duty here was about over and sent her home first. She had a boarding pass for the hospital's single light port. I needed separate passage in a light port to accommodate two, Song Bird and I. We will leave by the barn port."

Tall Willow kissed her on top of the head and then released her. "Good luck, Moon Dance. I am sorry that I have not had the privilege of meeting you and being friends till now. It is my loss."

"Thank you Damn Tall Willow. I needed your words as well as your arms tonight. Song Bird is one lucky woman. Go on, I am sure she has heard you humming and is waiting on you. I am going inside to pack my few Earth possessions. I will crawl out my bedroom window and leave the ranch after everyone goes to sleep. The winding Rattlesnake Rio calls to me. I will wander down and flow with it till I find a new body to enter. I will incarnate and start over again."

"Good Luck and may the Gods of Jupella watch over you till we meet again." He replied releasing her from his arms. "Wish me luck! I am off to hum and ask Song Bird to be my wife and go home with me."

"I am happy for you and Song Bird. Be happy!"

"I wish her grandsons felt the same. She is the Song Bird of my soul who makes me hum in the morning, noon, and night. Life without her, in my thinking, is unfathomable. She must go home with me."

"I should be so lucky." Moon Dance stated loudly as he walked away toward the barn. She immediately thought of Gray Feather, Jack Benson, and Charlie Elkhorn. All had abandoned her. She was so cold and numb on the inside. They had destroyed her. She suddenly felt a strange tingling in her left jaw. She wondered if her human body was getting ill, possibly developing a sore throat.

She walked back to the ranch house alone and entered the front door to avoid Charlie Elkhorn and his kitchen. She then made her way to her bedroom where, after entering, she locked the door behind her. She proceeded to gather up a few things for her journey. She would slip out into the night thru her bedroom window and walk away. With her bedroom door locked, Sleeping Moon's family would not miss her till breakfast time tomorrow. Somewhere out in the dark desert, she would unzip and discard Sleeping Moon's body. Then she would travel in spirit form till she found a vacant body to enter. She would choose wisely her next body and never trust another human male who told her that he loved her.

Meanwhile, out back inside the barn, Song Bird had rigged the door once more with a five gallon pail of bleach water. She could hear humming outside the barn as well as frightening humming coming from the loft of the barn. She wanted to run, but she felt trapped between the two. She desperately wanted to fall into Tall Willow's arms. She was in the barn because it was the night he promised to return to her. "Wait for me in the barn on hummer night" were his last words before Night Hawk had taken him from her, caged him in the horse trailer, and insisted John Mason put him in a nursing home for old cowboys and Indians. He was her lover and had been since her husband died. Her grandchildren did not understand her need and feelings for him.

Song Bird prepared for an unwanted intruder, possibly an alien by stretching the rope to the barn door handle taught. It had to be an alien. When he entered, she would yank the rope on the handle and the bucket of bleach water would drench the hummer alien as he stepped inside. She readied her grip on the rope because she could hear the humming now at the barn door. Then she saw the wooden plank door start to open. As a humming being stepped in, she jerked the rope on the door and the bucket of bleach water instantly fell drenching the figure in white.

"Oops!" Song Bird stated seeing who it was. She bit her lip.

"Why did you do that? Tall Willow asked between coughing, gagging and spitting. The bleach fumes were strong. "I took a shower with soap at the nursing home before coming here, damn it."

Song Bird grinned and then flew into his drenched wet arms.

CHAPTER SEVENTEEN

THE LAST GOODBYE

In the dark of Moon Dance's bedroom, she sat alone on the side of her bed staring at the dream catcher that had the pieces of her heart. Rising, she took the jar lid size dream catcher down and stored it in the pocket of her long Navajo skirt along with the small pistol that Night Hawk insisted she carry. Perhaps someday in a far off place, she might want to travel thru the port and take another peek at Gray Feather and his three babies that should be hers. She had no heart to love him anymore, but she was fascinated with the three tiny beings that looked just like him. She was an old fool and she knew it. After securing the tiny dream catcher in her pocket, she removed her pillow case to use for a tote bag. She then started to place in it necessities for a night's survival in the desert. It might be morning before she found a hidden spot to discard Sleeping Moon's body. She would need a shawl when the desert night air turned cold as well as a knife and a lighter to start a fire should she need to spend two days in the desert. She could eat Rattlesnake if necessary till she unzipped and moved on in spirit form. She wanted to check out the witch down by the Rio before she discarded her body. She was curious about the woman that Night Hawk was in love with, but had not met. It was one of those little things you cannot let go of before moving on. She had to know if the witch had three eyes and could possibly be a Weelo soul needing rescue.

As she stuffed a change of clothing into the pillowcase, she felt one of her arms tingle and try to go limp. In shock, she realized that the time had come. Sleeping Moon's body was dying. Continuing to pack was useless. She needed to leave now, make it into the edge of the desert, unzip, and discard Sleeping Moon's body.

Climbing out her bedroom window with one arm going numb wasn't easy, but she made it. The long, teal colored, cotton skirt she was wearing seemed to want to catch on everything. She pulled it loose from a splinter of wood on the window seal with her good arm. Her left arm was now useless. She had to hurry. If she had only a few hours as Sleeping Moon left, she wanted to live it in freedom and peace. If she lay a few hours or a few days dying in the desert, she was okay with that. She did not want assholes like Elkhorn staring, accusing her of being a demon, and watching her go. Outside the window in the dark, she straightened her clothing with her good arm. She then prepared to shuffle away into the shadows of the night. It wasn't going to be easy because her left leg was now tingling and feeling funny.

"Going somewhere?" a voice behind her in the dark asked startling her.

She turned quickly to see who the voice belonged to. Damn Tall Willow stood leaning against the Ranch house with tears in his eyes.

"I gather it did not go well with Song Bird; telling her you are not human." Moon Dance stated eyeing tears in the elderly man's eyes.

"She pulled her pistol on me when I unzipped this human face and let her see my purple one with three eyes. She yelled something about her being a good Catholic and that I had to be a Kachina demon who had been seducing her for years. She ran from me yelling she regretted every moment she had ever spent with me. My port came and I missed it. I was so busy arguing with Song Bird trying to make her understand who I am, that I missed my flight."

"Well, aren't we a pair!" Moon Dance stated shuffling over to him and putting her one good arm around him. She was feeling really cold and her one leg was refusing to move properly.

"What is wrong with your human arm?" He asked seeing it was limp.

"The body I am in is dying. I must find another to enter. I don't have long to live as Sleeping Moon and I don't want those in the house staring and watching me die and then unzipping this body and crawling out. I want this body to die in peace and me to exit and travel on in peace. My life here on the ranch has not been a pleasant one."

"I see. Suppose we both lay our bodies down. This body of mine is ninety-one. Would you like to incarnate together till we can manage to make it home? I will watch over you as your Earth body dies and help you unzip. Then, you do the same for me. I am willing to die from a Rattlesnake bite. My existence as Tall Willow is over. Song Bird doesn't want me!"

"Are you sure that you and Song Bird can't work it out?"

"No, you should have seen her face when I told her and showed her my purple skin and three eyes. She chose her Earth religion over me. Perhaps, I loved her more all of these years than she loved me. I proposed to her several times down thru the years. I see now that I was not number one in her life. This ranch, her religion, and her grandchildren come first. I am an old fool." He stated with a tear rolling down his cheek.

"I need you Tall Willow and welcome your willingness to incarnate with me. This human body known as Sleeping Moon is dying. I need you to hold me and help me walk into the desert, Tall Willow. One of my legs is going numb."

"I will hold you, Moon Dance, if you will hold me. I don't think I can exist without Song Bird. Like you, I may need to give the shattered pieces of my heart to the web."

Moon Dance hugged him with her one good arm. He put one arm around her shoulders securing her and with the other he reached down and scooped her legs up like she was a sleeping child that a father was carrying to bed. He then started walking towards the desert carrying her. Moon Dance put her one good arm around him. She felt secure in his arms even though her body, which was Sleeping Moon's, was cooling and growing numb.

"I need you Tall Willow. I don't think I can do another lifetime, another incarnation alone and unloved. Give the shattered pieces of your heart to me when you are ready. I will do my best to care for you and be there for you. I am not Song Bird, but I do need you and will be loyal to you."

"My life with Song Bird is over. My light port home is gone. You are what I have to cling to. If you will hold me, I will hold you till our souls can sing again." He kissed her on her forehead as he walked carrying her close to his heart.

Moon Dance could feel his heart beat. It was a good heartbeat, a loving one. Song Bird was a fool.

THE END

"MOON DANCE SLEEPS" is the second book in a series titled" ALIEN EN-
COUNTERS" by author Jo Hammers. The three book series titles are as follow

ALIEN ENCOUNTERS BOOK ONE – GRAY FEATHER'S FOG

ALIEN ENCOUNTERS BOOK TWO – MOON DANCE SLEEPS

ALIEN ENCOUNTERS BOOK THREE – NIGHT HAWK'S WITCH

www.ingramcontent.com/pod-product-compliance
Lightning Source LLC
Chambersburg PA
CBHW070603180626
46817CB00005B/1968